I0689752

FOO FIGHTERS

Also by Daniel Wyatt

Two Wings and a Prayer
Maximum Effort
The Last Flight of the Arrow
The Mary Jane Mission
The Cotton Run
Pennant Man
Route 66

"The Falcon File" series:
The Fuehrermaster
The Filberg Consortium
Foo Fighters

FOO FIGHTERS

The Falcon File 3

Daniel Wyatt

Published by
Bladud Books

Copyright © 2003, Daniel Wyatt

Daniel Wyatt has asserted his right under the Copyright, Designs and Patents Act, 1988, to be identified as the Author of this work.

First published in Great Britain in 2007 by Mushroom eBooks

This paperback edition published in 2018 by Bladud Books, an imprint of Mushroom Publishing, Bath, BA1 4EB, United Kingdom

www.bladudbooks.com

All rights reserved. No part of this publication may be reproduced in any form or by any means without the prior written permission of the publisher.

ISBN 978-1-84319-473-6

"Since I entered politics I have chiefly had men's views confided to me privately. Some of the biggest men in the United States, in the field of commerce and manufacture, are afraid of somebody, are afraid of something. They know that there is power somewhere so organized, so subtle, so watchful, so interlocked, so complete, so pervasive, that they had better not speak above their breath when they speak in condemnation of it."

Woodrow Wilson, 1913

Prologue

Henryk was desperate. He couldn't bear the thought of waiting until spring. He had lingered for this opportunity for days. *Was this it?* The armed SS guard at the front of the underground assembly line looked the other way, his back to the prisoners. Henryk glanced at the cave entrance. Darkness had covered the vast, mountainous terrain. He knew the artificial lighting beyond was somewhat dim in spots, mainly in the corners of the grounds. That would be to his advantage.

Another quick glance at the guard. . . then the entrance. . . the guard. . . then again at the entrance. He gulped.

Now!

Henryk took a breath and broke for the opening.

Once outside, he raced through the two inches of freshly fallen snow for the nearby, interim safety of the adjoining woods, one hundred feet off to the right. He stumbled once, got up, and ran even faster. A shot rang out. A second shot pinged off the gravel at his feet. Henryk didn't dare look back. He leaped the three-foot-high barbwire cleanly, and slid down the ravine in the darkness, grazing two trees as he went, bashing into a sharp, massive boulder at the bottom. He jumped up, slightly dazed, blood trickling out the corner of his mouth. He rubbed his face, licked the blood with his tongue, and looked around, brushing himself off. The moonlight dancing off the snow was bright enough to guide the prisoner's path.

South! He had to head south.

Switzerland. Where else? Make contact with the Americans. Or the

British. Wouldn't either of them—or both—love to get their hands on this place. The Russians? Piss on them! What did the Russians ever do for him? They were worse than the Nazis.

Polish prisoner Henryk Dubinsky would enjoy giving the right Allies the details of the underground project of the new radical Luftwaffe fighter-interceptor. If he could only get away. Henryk spoke German fluently. That was one plus. But his shaved head, lean body, hollow-eyes, and pale face would give him away as a prisoner. How far would he get in the snow and cold without a thicker coat than the one he was wearing? He had a few hundred kilometres to go to reach the Swiss border. He'd have to take that chance. Anything was better than what went on. . . in the cave.

At the bottom of the hill, he got his bearings and turned to what he took to be the general direction of south. . . and freedom. *Switzerland.* Where there would be some semblance of normal life, again, like peaceful, uncomplicated pre-war Poland. Back in the tunnel, all hell had to be breaking loose. Someone—a guard or two—would undoubtedly be shot for incompetence.

Then dog barks pierced the night air.

So soon?

Run, you fool. . . run. . . run. . .

4

One

Donovan needed time to think.

He twirled his padded chair ninety degrees into the sunshine streaming through the open vertical window blinds. A car horn honked down at street level. Today's first-thing-in-the-morning phone call from the White House hadn't surprised him. Orders were orders. Besides, every boss had a boss too. Such was politics in the nation's capital.

OSS Director Bill Donovan had been witness to four years of drastic changes in his business, in this the sixth year of war. The intelligence agency had evolved from its first rather silly label of Coordinator of Information by a 1941 presidential order, to the present day OSS—Office of Strategic Services—a year later. With only ninety-two people to kick-start it in 1942, the OSS now deployed 16,000 members worldwide, many of those engaged in clandestine operations behind enemy lines. All this out of Donovan's headquarters here at 2430 E Street in the nation's capital, where his door was said to be always open to anyone.

Donovan had tolerated the earlier mass of confusion in setting the secret force up.

The recruiting.

The hiring.

The colourful figures. Actors. Poets. Lawyers. Bankers. Filmmakers.

In time came the stress. The countless hours in the office after midnight. He had also put up with the jokes on what the OSS stood for. *Oh, so sweet. Oh, so social. Oh, so stupid.* They were often accused of fighting a plush war. But only the jealous said such things, and in whispers.

5

Major-General William "Wild Bill" Donovan was a vigorous sixty-one years young. Most men would consider retirement at his tender age, after such a flamboyant career as Wall Street lawyer, decorated World War I battlefield hero, Republican nominee for New York Governor, and OSS Director. But this modern knight of the twentieth century had no intention to retire from public service. He still had a mission to fulfil, and that was to see the end of the war, the war that saw the OSS conduct subversion, propaganda, and extensive military operations to confuse America's enemies. This was the war that made Donovan the man of the hour in Washington, the nation's number one information gatherer. In Washington, hordes were talking about Bill Donovan and his activities. The organization that he had pieced together from nothing in 1941 was now more powerful and more influential than the FBI. And certain people cringed at that, namely FBI Director J. Edgar Hoover. Financed by secret funds at his disposal, with minimal security and little red tape to bother with, the OSS was a law unto itself, the way Donovan and President Roosevelt preferred it. The less the public knew, the better.

The President. Bless him.

Now there was a sad case, Donovan thought painfully.

Donovan chuckled, his memory selecting one particular White House visit in 1943, when he had pulled a fast one on his vigilant commander-in-chief. The general, by then a common visitor to the mansion on 1600 Pennsylvania Avenue, had approached the Oval Office carrying a sandbag and a concealed weapon, a new, noiseless, flashless .22-calibre pistol. Roosevelt, dictating a letter to his secretary, waved for Donovan to enter the room. While Roosevelt and the woman were preoccupied, Donovan set the sandbag on the floor, then quickly fired an entire clip of bullets into it. Neither Roosevelt nor his secretary so much as flinched. When the secretary left the room, Donovan wrapped the hot barrel with a handkerchief and presented the silent killer gun to the startled president, who hadn't heard a thing.

"Wild Bill," the president had roared after the incident, "you're the only black Republican I'll ever allow in my office with a weapon like this. Give my regards to the manufacturer."

Donovan did just that. He also placed an order for several of the guns for his OSS people.

Those were the last of the fun-loving days at the White House. Roosevelt was a different man in 1945—with little spark left in him now. He was sick and he was stubborn. And he wanted to travel halfway around the world to meet with Churchill and Stalin at Yalta, the third of the conferences between the influential Allied leaders who held all the cards in a stacked deck. Furthermore, he wanted to check in with the Kid, Wesley Hollinger.

The general nodded to himself. He played with the lapel of his military-style uniform, then punched his intercom button. *Figures.* Especially after some of the crazy rumours coming out of Germany, via his OSS men and women. Yes, Hollinger was the right choice. He'd keep his mouth shut.

A woman's voice broke the silence. "Yes, General."

"Get me London on the phone," he demanded. "The SI branch."

"Yes, sir. I'll get right on it."

ALDERHORST, GERMANY

Martin Bormann was the acting Deputy Fuehrer since Rudolf Hess had flown off on his crazy peace mission to Scotland in 1941.

The Nazi leaders had many names for this short, thick set, bull neck man with the bulbous nose and beer-belly stomach. The Brown Eminence. The Executor. Herr Moneybags. The Shadow. The Little Fat Man. The Boot-licker. The Kiss-Ass. The Pig. The Skirt-chaser. Every name seemed to fit. And more. Only the kindest of voices called him an opportunist. Earlier in the war, Luftwaffe Reichmarshall Hermann Goering once went so far as to say that he hoped that Bormann would rot in hell one day soon! Others in authority echoed Goering's remarks.

Martin Bormann was Adolf Hitler's personal secretary, answerable only to the Fuehrer. Bormann was the mystery person. He toiled in the shadows as Hitler's spokesman, carrying with him the important title of Reichsleiter. Feared by the other Nazi leaders, he secured his position by hanging onto Hitler's coattails, while remaining virtually unknown in the public eye. Unlike Hermann Goering and others, titles meant nothing to the forty-four-year old Bormann. Power was everything. To reach Hitler, one had to go through Bormann first. Few people in the Nazi party knew that Bormann was the real builder of Hitler's Bavarian mountain resort, Berghof. As Hitler's trustee, it was

Bormann who had expropriated surrounding farms and forests, and had laid out the roads and the buildings for the estate. And just that morning Bormann had hoodwinked Hitler into signing the paperwork for Bormann to access the Swiss bank accounts of Heinrich Himmler, Hermann Goering, and other notables in the event of their deaths. They didn't call Bormann "the Executor" for nothing. They were quite the duo, Hitler and Bormann. The Little Corporal and the Little Fat Man.

As the war had dragged on and Germany had lost ground, Hitler became occupied more with military affairs, leaving the internal party matters to Bormann. This was where the true strength and power lay. And Bormann knew it. It was the Party. This afternoon in his hut next to Hitler's, Bormann was scribbling on his writing pad. He was dressed in his favourite attire, Reichsleiter uniform consisting of reddish-brown service tunic, gold-braided red armband adorned with black swastika, gold insignia featuring his rank on the collar flaps, tight riding breeches and glossy-black riding boots.

"Bormann!" the Fuehrer shouted from next door.

Bormann bounced to his feet, trotting around the corner, his daily log—his *tagebuch*—in hand. "Yes, mein Fuehrer."

"Close the door, Bormann," Hitler ordered, his voice laboured and raspy. "I need to have a word with you."

"Yes, mein Fuehrer."

Hitler was pacing the floor, slowly, stooped over. "We have no choice but to make haste to Berlin. There we will make our final stand. Is the Fuehrerbunker at the Chancellery ready?"

Bormann hadn't expected the move so soon. "They are putting the finishing touches to it as we speak, mein Fuehrer."

"How much longer?"

"One week, mein Fuehrer."

"Make the arrangements. I am too busy with other matters."

The order didn't sound too difficult to Bormann. "Certainly, mein Fuehrer." Bormann knew what matters those were—tending to the mighty Russian Red Army knocking at Hitler's door in the snow only a few miles away. For weeks Bormann had received only scant attention from the Fuehrer, so now was a good time to ask about the idea he had been toying with.

"Mein Fuehrer?"

"Yes?"

"May I have your permission to see my wife for a few days? I promise to be back in time for the move to Berlin."

With listless eyes, Hitler stared at his secretary for a long period. "Yes, go ahead. You deserve it. Gerda is a good woman. Spend some time with her." He tore at an individually-wrapped chocolate and popped it in his mouth.

"Thank you, mein Fuehrer."

Hitler grunted, plunking himself down in his chair. His shaky hand went out to his loyal Alsatian dog, Blondi. Only twenty minutes out of bed, the Fuehrer's face was ashen. For months he had taken to being moody, with frequent fits of rage. He was a recluse. Dependent on drugs, he was sleeping in until early afternoon every day. The rest of the time he was a walking skeleton, his clothes drooping on him. Bormann thought it pathetic how the Fuehrer was fighting a war on words only, now that his 1945 empire was a mere one-tenth the size it was during its peak in late 1941, when all Europe trembled at the sight and sound of Nazi jackboots. No more.

"Everyone has turned against me. My generals! Some generals! We had the strongest army on earth. We had Moscow in our sights. We had control of the continent. My backers! They were the worst! They were the true traitors. They deserted me."

"Are you referring to the group?"

Hitler patted his dog. "Yes, Bormann. Of course, the group!" he shouted, trying to sustain the anger in his voice, and failing. "And to think some of them were Americans. Prominent Americans who expected favours. Wall Street money. They only wanted me to dig Germany and Europe out of the Depression. They didn't want to see the misery spread elsewhere. Europe needed a leader. And I was it. I had great and wonderful designs for a new Europe. So did they. They agreed to it. A united Europe with a common currency, a central bank. My Council of Peace. A European Economic Community that would include Great Britain, had they so wished. Then they decided I was no longer useful to them. They sold me out." Hitler breathed a sigh.

"Yes, they did, mein Fuehrer." Bormann had heard his leader explode about this same subject only four days before. You can't fight the people who sign the checks, Mein Fuehrer, he thought.

9

"They left me and Germany on our own," Hitler continued, intoxicated at the sound of his voice. "Those rich Jews in the group engineered this act of treachery. George Washington once said that it is better to be alone than be in bad company. Britain was my friend. My ally. I sought peace with them. We could have had a great future in alliance with Britain. They could have kept their sea power, leaving us with the continent. That was the arrangement. Crush the Russians! The hordes of the east. Then that bastard Churchill came along to spoil everything."

"Yes, he surely did, mein Fuehrer."

"*Mein Kampf* was written in vain. England was our friend, and we fought them. So useless. Oh, so useless. But we still have our secret weapons. But there's more. Our scientists and their machines will turn the tide where our imbecile generals have failed."

Bormann smiled. "You are absolutely right, mein Fuehrer, as usual."

Hitler rose to his feet, a sudden quickness to his movements. "I know I'm right! Go, now. See your wife. I have to attend a military conference. Go, but hurry back."

"Of course, mein Fuehrer." Bormann stood in an instant. "I will always be your humble servant."

"Yes, yes. Give my compliments to your dear wife."

"I will, mein Fuehrer. And she will give you hers, I'm sure."

Hitler smiled, sadly, lost in something else for the moment.

Bormann clicked his heels and excused himself. At his office, he wrote down what he had remembered Hitler had said to him, a ritual that the secretary had started that week. Recording every word uttered from the Fuehrer's mouth in his daily log was one way to keep his mind occupied and off smoking, which he had quit at Christmas. It was also for posterity, for future generations.

Near Hamburg, Germany

Word had come down. Zerstorer Unit 22 had their assignment.

An hour after sundown, two men in overalls slid back the long, steel-plated hangar door at Loebitz airfield. Two more men joined them and began the task of rolling out and positioning the strange, shiny fighters on the outside concrete.

Six machines in total.

Finished, the four men stood back in awe. These fighters were an odd, distinct shape, smaller than the Messerschmitt BF-109s on the far side of the airfield. Each machine had an undercarriage, complete with tires. It had wings, if you could call them wings, and a long nozzle poking out the nose. But there was no room for a pilot aboard. Too tiny, for one thing. Besides, there was no access to the cockpit. These same four men were told by their superiors when the machines arrived the day before that this was Germany's new, revolutionary fighter-interceptor that would change the course of the war.

This was the V-4—designated the Messerschmitt V-4 Experimental Series 1-1a—fourth in the series of the vengeance weapons.

The four men relaxed, lit cigarettes in the night air, and waited for the voice prompt from the tower. The sergeant in charge looked to the starry sky, devoid of any Allied bombers for the moment. But they'd be coming on schedule. As sure as the sun rises in the east.

Soon. In minutes, probably.

"Do you think these things will actually work?" one of the men said.

The sergeant dragged on his cigarette, delaying his answer. "It'll be. . . interesting." He nodded. "Yes, they'll work."

"I wish I could be up there to see them perform."

"Me, too. You know, I have an idea." The sergeant grinned. "Why not strap yourself to one of them?"

"Hey, don't pass that around. Our superiors may ask someone to do it."

The men laughed in agreement, their voices echoing off the hangar.

"Yes, you may be right."

"I know I'm right."

Two

Wesley Hollinger got up fifteen minutes before the alarm could scream in his ear and kissed his wife on the cheek. No response. Then he shuffled his way to the bathroom, careful not to wake her. She needed her rest more than ever in her present pregnant state. Quietly as he could, he found his shaving brush in the medicine cabinet and lathered his face. He sighed, grabbed for the razor and began the routine.

"Ouch!"

"Sliced yourself again?"

Hollinger saw his wife at the door. "What are you doing? I thought you were sleeping."

"Good grief." Roberta tied her nightgown at her waist. "How can I, with the racket in here."

Hollinger grabbed a piece of toilet paper to stop the bleeding on his chin and looked in the mirror. "Sorry." Roberta never ceased to amaze him. She could climb out of bed first thing in the morning and still look like a million bucks.

She smiled, and stepped forward, hugging her husband from behind, kissing his neck, her long, shiny, red hair falling on his bare back. "Don't flatter me."

"Going into work today?" he asked, his voice soft.

"Later."

"How'd you manage that?"

"I cleared it with the colonel."

"Pull, huh?"

13

"Bloody damn right, Yank."

He returned a smile, eyeing her in the mirror, while pressing the toilet paper to his skin. Under her floor-length nightgown, Roberta was a slim, brown-eyed, slender-nosed, extremely attractive English woman moored on thin but sturdy legs. She kissed him on the neck.

"And what, pray-tell, is that for?" he asked.

"I love you."

"Normally, I'd return the favour and plant one. But I don't want to smear blood all over your face."

The young couple giggled.

She let go of him and stood sideways before the mirror. "Look."

"What?" Hollinger continued shaving.

"Me, dummy." She stroked her stomach.

"So?"

"I feel so bloated."

"Come on, Robbie. You can't even tell," he teased her.

"I can."

"Well, yeah, maybe a bit. Looks like you had an extra serving at the table."

"*Thanks.*"

"You're welcome." He slapped her on the rump.

"Hey!" She turned and slapped him hard on the back, then grabbed him.

"No, don't!" he screamed. "We promised. Remember, no tickling! We made a pact."

"I just broke it."

"No!"

Laughing, he pinned her left arm to the wall and kissed her hard on the mouth, while she ran her free hand through his long, wavy hair.

"There, now you have blood on your face," he said.

Four months into her pregnancy, Roberta Langford-Hollinger had been able to hide her condition so far, except for her fuller face. Her regular clothes still fit her, for now. According to her doctor everything was going fine. Despite some occasional morning sickness, Roberta told her husband and the doctor that she felt healthy enough. She was eating regular meals, without throwing up, and she had quit smoking.

After breakfast of toast and strong, imported American coffee, Hollinger quick-kissed his wife goodbye, donned his coat, left the third-story apartment with an umbrella, and strode the five blocks in the light, chilly rain to OSS headquarters on Grosvenor Street, only a few doors down from General Eisenhower's Supreme Headquarters Allied Expeditionary Force.

Along the way, Hollinger recalled his first sight of London. It was the fall of 1940, in the middle of the Blitz, when the city and the country had stood alone against Hitler. Hollinger was one of the first American Intelligence agents to arrive—new, green, impressionable, and single. Back home in the States, he had remembered the cool, calm, much-in-command radio voice of CBS's Edward Murrow, broadcasting live from the war-torn city to millions of Americans, as if it were yesterday:

"This. . . is London. Trafalgar Square. The noise that you hear at the moment is the sound of an air raid siren. I'm standing here just on the steps of St Martin's in the Field. It's almost impossible to realize that men are killing and being killed, even when you see that ever-thickening streak of smoke pouring down from the sky which means a plane and perhaps several men are going down in flames. The sense of danger, death, and disaster comes only when the familiar incidents occur. The sight of half a dozen ambulances weighted down with an unseen cargo of human wreckage has jarred me more than the roar of dive bombers or the sounds of bombs. But London has gotten used to it. A near miss rocked the cab I was in one evening. The old man slid back the window and remarked, 'You know, sir, Hitler'll do that once too often, once.'"

Everything had changed in the five years since the awful Blitz. Hitler did do it once too often. The hunter had now become the hunted.

At the office, Hollinger dove into the papers his efficient, forty-year-old American secretary brought to him in a locked briefcase. Wesley Hollinger was a blue-eyed, six-foot, trim-as-an-athlete, twenty-seven-year old OSS agent, with a fetish for expensive custom suits and wide-brimmed fedoras. The ruggedly-handsome, hot-rock agent had worked his way up to second-in-command of the OSS Secret Intelligence branch—the SI—in mid-1944. Since then, he had been given his own secretary, who this morning had briefed him on information of the much-heralded German secret arsenal of weapons deployed against the Allies. The information included several fast jet and rocket aircraft, the deadly V-1 pilotless flying bomb, and the even-deadlier V-2 intercontinental rocket. With the war drawing to a close, the SI's mission

15

was to obtain all the data it could on the subject of Nazi secret weapons. So far, the OSS agents were doing their job in enemy territory, substantiated by the photographs and hand-drawn maps of the locations of these assembly sites in the file at his fingertips.

Hollinger looked it over until the desk telephone rang. He lifted the receiver, slowly. "Hollinger here."

"Wesley. I want to see you. Pronto."

"Yes, sir."

Hollinger took to the main hall and ducked through the white-lettered oak door marked SI DIRECTOR, where Jack Dorwin was behind his desk. In his thirty-eighth year, Dorwin was a heavy-set man, built along the lines of an overweight football player. His face resembled a horse's: long, with flaring nostrils. This morning his flowery red tie was too bright and his shirt too tight in the mid-section. He was one of the worst-dressed Americans at the OSS London headquarters.

"What happened to you?" Dorwin asked, looking up, inhaling a long cigar, pushing aside the memorandums in his OUT basket. He had the tired eyes of a typical overworked, stressed-out American.

"Cut myself shaving. You're only the fifth one who asked."

"Close the door, Wesley."

"Yes, sir."

"How's that redhead wife of yours?"

"Still red. So far, so good. She's coming along. Doesn't show yet."

"She will, quickly enough. Sit down, boy."

"Thank you, sir. What's up?"

"Here. Open it." Dorwin slid an envelope across his desk. He stabbed his intercom box button. "Mrs. Cellborth?" he called his secretary.

"Yes, sir."

"Would you please ask statistics for the B-49 log? In the meantime, Mr. Hollinger and I do not want to be disturbed."

"As you wish, sir."

"What's this?" Hollinger wanted to know, spreading the envelope flaps.

"Orders from the boss."

"Which one? I've got quite a few."

"The man in Washington."

"Donovan?"

"No, Roosevelt."

"The president?" Hollinger began to read the text.

Dorwin nodded. "You're going to rendezvous with the old man. He's meeting with Churchill and Stalin. Son of a gun, boy, you must have kissed somebody's fat ass at the capital."

"Hell, I haven't seen Roosevelt in a good three years." Hollinger jabbed the paper with his finger. "By the way, where's this Yalta place?"

"Crimea. On the Black Sea. The Soviet Union."

"Oh, the Soviet Union." Hollinger began to calculate in his mind as best he could how many miles that would be. *Let's see.* Too many for him. That meant flying. He hated flying.

"I hear it's warm there all year round. Like Florida. Palm trees. You'll probably see some beautiful Russian women in bathing suits."

Hollinger folded his arms. "Beautiful women, eh? In that case I had better check with the powers-that-be on this one."

Dorwin frowned. "Who? Donovan?"

"No. My wife."

Dorwin chuckled through widely-spaced teeth. He leaned forward, elbows on his desk, cigar clutched between the fingers of his right hand. "Let me give you some advice, Wesley. A little word to the wise."

"Wise to the wise, is it? I'm listening, as always, sir."

The director scribbled something on his blotter, then looked up. "My hunch on this is that your little Crimean get-together with Roosevelt has something to do with our research and collecting of information, if you know what I mean."

Hollinger nodded. "I think I get your drift. German Secret Weapons."

"Yes. Furthermore, let me say that we have here what the OSS calls a *situation.* You're representing the SI and the OSS first, and not necessarily the will of the president. Our work is classified."

Something didn't sit right in Hollinger's craw. "But. . . but, sir. . . he's. . . the president."

"That don't mean shit, boy. We don't want anything leaking to the wrong people. Fact is, the OSS doesn't quite trust some people close to Roosevelt. Another thing, he's not quite himself, I hear."

"Why is he not himself?"

"Trust me on this one."

Hollinger held his boss's stare as long as he could. "Yes, sir. I understand." *I suppose.*

Sergeant Arthur Benjamin Tooney of Jamestown, North Dakota bent down and slowly grabbed the brace that attached the turret to the fuselage. With the other hand he pulled the gun-elevation hand crank away from the holding clip and placed it in the socket. Then he released the brake and cranked the turret so that the guns dropped from aft to a ninety-degree elevation. He held the hand crank in position, reached over and unlocked the door, swung it open, and braked the turret's position from the inside.

Tooney immediately heard the whistling slipstream and felt a strong draft. He flipped his goggles down over his eyes. Through the round, thirteen-inch-diameter viewing glass, he was able to catch a clear glimpse of the eerie North Sea below, and the sunlight blinking off the white caps. Then he stood up, gripped the brace, and eased down into the turret by placing the left foot on the seat and his right foot on the stirrup. Next, he spread his legs out on the footrests on either side of the window and dropped his five-foot-five, one hundred and forty pound frame onto the armoured seat. He glanced up and gestured to the waist gunner, who handed Tooney his parachute, before slam-locking the turret from the inside.

Sergeant Tooney was now alone, suspended at the bottom of the B-17 Flying Fortress bomber *Lady Luck*, cramped into the foetal position. The only sounds were the steady drone of his bomber's four radial engines and the thundering slipstream. It was a perfect three hundred and sixty degree view inside the ball turret, which he called *the best seat in the house.*

He spread out on the small seat as best he could in the confined space in his bulky, fleece-lined flight gear. He scanned the blue sky through the Plexiglas. It was a bright, sunny day above scattered thick, white clouds.

He flicked on the main power switch, and charged the guns by yanking back on the handles. Then he pressed the fire selector switch. By deploying the two joysticks in front of his face, Tooney controlled the movement of the hydraulically-powered turret. He spun the machine upright, then around, back and forth to check the field of fire. The turret whined and whirred in his ears.

A voice crackled over his earphone. . .

"PILOT TO BALL GUNNER. HOW DOES IT LOOK BACK THERE? ANY GAPS IN THE LOWER FORMATION?"

Tooney pinched his throat intercom button. "NOT A ONE, SIR. THE OTHER GROUP IS BANKED RIGHT ON OUR BEHIND."

"THANKS. PILOT OUT."

The bomber nosed up and climbed, the engines straining.

It was an impressive sight to Sergeant Tooney. He could see the other four-engine heavies jockeying for position, part of an American bomber stream of B-17s heading with purpose to Magdeburg, Germany, arranged in their respective groups and wings. Upper, mid, and low squadrons. Over three-hundred Big Ass Birds carrying high-explosive payloads, escorted by friendly P-51 Mustangs. From this vantage point he could see everything better than the tail gunner. He could tell who the good pilots were, and who were the so-so's, and which squadron or group ran a tight formation or not. Gosh, she was a beautiful thing to behold for the nineteen-year-old prairie boy. He wondered how many other green crews out there in the wide blue yonder were on their first mission, like his crew was, with a brand-spanking new B-17G fresh from the Boeing factory in the States to play with.

"PILOT TO CREW. TEN THOUSAND FEET. PUT OXYGEN MASKS ON."

Tooney wrapped the rubber piece around his mouth and studied the oxygen indicator beside him. Four hundred pounds pressure. He reached under his seat to plug in his heated flying suit.

"PILOT TO GUNNERS. TEST YOUR GUNS."

Sergeant Tooney gripped the handles of his twin Browning .50-calibre guns, his peashooters, as he referred to them. He had 250 rounds for each gun at his disposal—five armour piercing shells to one tracer—each gun preset to the thirty-two-foot wingspan of an ME-109. Accurate range of the guns at best were six hundred yards, although they were still deadly at one thousand yards. He fired three short bursts, deafened by the sound of his own guns. . . and saw the all-important tracers.

He sniffed. The smell of cordite hung heavy in the cold air, cutting through his rubber mask.

HAMBURG

The civilian radar technician attached to Zerstorer Unit 22 picked up the blips on the screen as soon as they were of height over the North

Sea, east of the East Anglia coast, and wasted no time in waving his supervisor over.

"What is it, Wolfgang?"

"Here they come in force, Herr Leyberger."

"How many?" the supervisor asked.

"I'd guess two hundred to three hundred. Thirteen thousand feet on a heading of one-one-zero degrees."

Visibly pleased, Leyberger tapped his technician on the shoulder. "Excellent. I will send out the alert to Loebitz airfield."

OVER THE NORTH SEA

At exactly 1105 hours, the bomber formation climbed. . . then levelled out. In the sub-stratosphere, condensation trails began to form off the engines in the stream. In *Lady Luck*'s belly, Tooney could feel every move and jitter of the aircraft. Despite the sun peering over his right shoulder, he started to feel the intense cold on his face. Small lines of frost formed on the Plexiglas window at his feet, but, thankfully, not enough to blur his vision. He wiggled his toes in his boots, and pulled his insulated cap down closer to his eyebrows. It was going to get chilly.

"NAVIGATOR TO PILOT. ENEMY COAST COMING. . . IN TWO MINUTES."

"ROGER."

"WE SHOULDN'T EXPECT ANY FLAK. NOT IN THIS CLOUD."

"WE HOPE. PILOT OUT."

Tooney looked down at a jagged light-brown crease outlined by white surf. The coast. Tooney spotted snow and ground patches below. This was not friendly territory. He was over Germany for the first time in his life. His stomach tightened. He was in the presence of the enemy, in the range of their radar, their fighters, and their anti-aircraft guns.

"PILOT TO CREW. KEEP YOUR EYES OPEN FOR FIGHTERS."

Sergeant Tooney saw a set of specks off to his right, appearing to move crosswise into the bomber formation. Distance, a few miles. They were closing. Fast! He remembered the flashcard images of German fighters and aircraft identification exercises back at the base. This was no drill. This was the real thing.

He counted the objects.

Two. . . four. . . six. . .

He pinched his throat mike. "BALL GUNNER TO PILOT. I SEE A BUNCH OF FIGHTERS. EIGHT O'CLOCK LEVEL. COMING STRAIGHT FOR US!"

"CALM DOWN. BE SPECIFIC," the pilot, the crew's voice of discipline, said. "WHAT ARE THEY? HOW MANY? ARE THEY OURS?"

"FOCKE-WULF 190'S, SIR. TEN. . . NO TWELVE. HERE THEY COME!"

Tooney went for his gun grips, but all twelve enemy fighters rolled over and flew by flat out, too rapidly for him to even get away a single round. He cursed under his breath. Gunner training back home over the Gulf of Mexico was never like this. He glanced to the side. They were heading for the low squadrons.

Two more ferocious attacks came and went. Six fighters, in pairs, diving out of the sun, each with spurts of flames flashing off their wing guns. Then nothing. Where'd they go? Tooney relaxed and watched the formation breaking up the puffy clouds. Then he saw something. . . a strange object coming up swiftly, then remaining at a distance of two-hundred yards, weaving in and out of the clouds. It was shiny. Small, wide wings. Lump of a cockpit. What the blazes! He couldn't recall any enemy flashcard image like this.

"BALL GUNNER TO PILOT. WE HAVE COMPANY. FIVE O'CLOCK LOW."

"BE SPECIFIC."

"I DON'T KNOW WHAT THE HELL IT IS." He cocked his guns, trying to bear down on the incoming. . . whatever it was. *Remember, short bursts. Forget it. Too fast.* "LOOK AT IT GO! SHE'S COMING UNDER. THERE IT GOES!"

"TAIL GUNNER TO PILOT. I SAW IT TOO, SIR."

"WHAT WAS IT?"

"HELL IF I KNOW, SIR."

"WHAT'S WITH YOU GUYS? DID IT SHOOT?"

"NO."

"THEN MAYBE SHE'S ONE OF OURS. PILOT TO ALL GUNNERS. KEEP A LOOKOUT FOR ANY MORE."

Tooney pressed his intercom button. "I WILL, SIR."

What the hell was it?

NORTHERN COAST OF THE ANTARCTIC PENINSULA

Inside the small cabin of U-344, the scientist held up his right hand in a Nazi salute, his left hand clutching a copy of Adolf Hitler's bestselling book, *Mein Kampf*. He took a breath of the musty air, mixed with an acid smell of diesel fuel. It had been a long, boring sub trip since leaving Hamburg, except for the stopover in Argentina to refuel. Those two days in Rio was something, even for a married man like him.

"With your left hand on the divine word, you will read the oath from the sheet, please," the sub skipper explained, holding up a typed piece of paper for the scientist to read.

It seemed odd to the scientist to be initiated by such a young man. The sub skipper—Manfred Stoeller—was, maybe, thirty. If that. Twenty-five or twenty-six was more like it.

The scientist cleared his throat and began. *"I, Otto Bauer, of my own free will and accord, and under the threat of my own death, solemnly and sincerely swear that I will always secretly hail and henceforth never reveal the cherished mysteries of the Order of the Knights of National Socialism and our ruler, the Commander Fuehrer, to the profane, those who are not chosen to stand by us in our global struggle. I furthermore promise and swear that I will protect any and every fellow blood brother of the Order of the Knights of National Socialism from the profane who seek to pervert or destroy our hallowed Order so help me the most excellent and worshipful lord of this world. Hail Commander Fuehrer and his divine wisdom."*

Stoeller snatched the sheet from the scientist as they exchanged glances. "Otto Bauer, you are now a brother to the first degree of the Order of the Knights of National Socialism. Welcome to the elite fraternity."

"Thank you."

The two whiskered men bowed to each other, clicking their heels. The sub skipper reached into a desk drawer, pulled out a shiny medallion, the size of a large coin, and gave it to Bauer. The scientist fingered it. It was heavy, made of gold. Engraved on it was an ancient Roman soldier on horseback, with sword in hand, holding a Swastika flag, above it the letters KNS.

"Thank you, Lieutenant Stoeller."

"And, of course, this." Stoeller carefully handed over a bright red sash. Embroidered on it was a black swastika on a white circle. "Wear them on your person when you meet secretly with other brothers of the Order."

"I will be delighted, Lieutenant Stoeller."

"Remember, I shall return in three months. At that time I will take you on an extraordinary journey."

"Where, may I dare ask?"

"Under the Antarctic icecap."

"*Under* the icecap? Are you serious?"

"Quite serious. Keep that to yourself. It's your first closely-guarded secret of the Order. So is Neuschwabenland."

"What is that?"

"The Fatherland's territory already staked out here. Now, you must go. Your party on the surface awaits you. Heil Hitler."

For centuries, men only suspected that Antarctica existed. The Romans and early Greeks wrote of it. The Romans called it *Terra incognita australis*, meaning unknown southern land. New Zealand tribes spoke of the great white land to the south. In the early nineteenth century, whalers of many countries combed the nearby waters, but kept their hunting grounds secret. Then in 1838, United States Navy Lieutenant Charles Wilkes saw enough of the region to confirm that the Antarctic did exist, and in fact was a massive continent of ice, snow, and murderous weather. In 1911, Norwegian explorers reached the centre of the great landmass, and hence were the first to stand on the South Pole. Then, after thirty years of expeditions conducted by various countries, rumours leaked out in 1940 that the unknown continent contained important minerals. The Germans were there to see if the rumours were true.

It was a sharp change for Otto Bauer, going from the depths of the chugging, diesel-powered submarine to the startling outside. *Why here?* he thought, as he and the sailor left the sub behind and began to row the rubber raft to the nearby shore under a grey overcast.

Outfitted in fur-lined parkas, pants, boots, and mittens, they were dressed for the conditions. It was a few degrees below zero. The water was calm, not a breath of wind. The shore was shrouded in a ground mist. *Couldn't they find a warmer place to dig? Like Africa?* Lots of minerals in Africa. Tons of them. He didn't want to come here. But one part of him welcomed the challenge. Better than the rubble and ashes of beleaguered Germany. After a short time, the scientist flipped down his hood and looked out upon the glacial waters of the Antarctic Ocean, intermingled with a few large chunks of flat ice. Bauer shot a glance back to the open water where U-344 was fast disappearing in the fog, his last link to the Fatherland severed.

Fifty yards from shore, the scientist could make out patches of bare rock shimmering through the mist. The stark wasteland gripped him, leaving him empty. This was awful country. For a moment his mind flashed to home, then von Braun at Peenemunde, and finally his two Arab horses boarded away in Switzerland, in a safe haven. He jerked his head at the sound of a shout that drifted across the water. A figure appeared, waving. To the far right, up from the water, was a jeep. The sailor waved back. They continued rowing, closer and closer to land, their breath steaming in the frigid air. Now in clear, shallow water, Bauer saw rocks below the surface. They pulled onto thick gravel. Bauer looked about. To his surprise, he managed to identify some lichens and mosses a few feet away. Life! There was plant life here.

"Thank you," the scientist said to his rower, steering onto shore.

"Good luck." The sailor handed the two pieces of heavy gear to Bauer, then took to the icy waters once again with a splash.

"Heil Hitler."

"Heil Hitler!" the sailor replied, enthusiastically.

Bauer turned to the figure he had seen earlier. He was a stout man, full-bearded face, with hardened, wind-burned skin. A man his age. This was more like it, thought the scientist. Someone past forty. At last, someone who remembered vividly Germany before Hitler, not like the wet-behind-the-ears kids on the sub. "Herr Raeder? Wilhelm Raeder?"

"Yes. Otto Bauer?"

"At your service, Herr Raeder."

"How is my friend, Wernher?" The man was well-spoken, his voice as clean and sharp as the Antarctic air.

"Excellent. He sends his regards with a bottle of French wine—1934."

"Ah, the best. Good old Wernher."

They shook hands first, then broke into abbreviated Nazi salutes. Raeder smiled.

"Welcome to summer in the Antarctic."

"Thank you."

"It is twenty-four degrees Fahrenheit. One of our warmer days this week. Two weeks ago, the thermometer reached forty."

Bauer grinned. "In that case, Herr Raeder, I should have brought my swimsuit."

"Don't worry," Raeder had to laugh. "We've got extras, should you require one. Hand me your bags. By the way, Otto, we use only first names here. And we don't salute."

In the jeep, during the six-kilometre jaunt to camp, Raeder, the chief geologist of the German mineral expedition to Antarctica, filled Bauer in, as he drove slowly over the tracks he had made fifteen minutes before. "This time of year—the summer—is more conducive to mining, and we've been taking advantage of it. We've uncovered a huge deposit of coal, and traces of oil, copper, lead, zinc. However, many of the deposits are low-grade. Another drawback is drilling through the ice, snow, and rock. We've had heavy-duty equipment sent to us by cargo ship a week ago. We're already using it. We're progressing much faster now."

"What about light metals? Magnesium? Aluminium?"

"Nothing... yet. But we're still looking."

Bauer nodded, disappointed at the lacklustre news. Precious light metals in Antarctica still sounded too far-fetched to him.

Raeder drove through the mountain pass, into a flat lowland of white, nestled below a sharp ridge. "There she is. Camp Berlin."

Bauer put his binoculars to his eyes. His throat tightened, taking it all in. "*Mein Gott!*" The scientist was amazed. Clustered together like a small town were tents and clapboard structures of various sizes. Two tents supported Swastika flags. Then his eyes fell on what appeared to be... telephone poles!

"We have our own power station. The big hut in the middle. Short-wave radio, electricity, oil heating, all the conveniences of home. Up there, in the hills to the right, is one part of our drilling operation."

Bauer observed the ridge, returning his view to Camp Berlin itself. "Quite the place," was all he could say until they drove the last two kilometres to the site.

Reader slammed on the brakes in the centre of the huts, below a large sign on a four-by-four post that read SOUTH POLE 2,565 KILO-METRES. "Are you hungry, Otto?"

"Yes, I do believe I am."

"Out we go. I'll get someone to settle you in. Then I'll join you for a meal before we set off to our first drilling site."

"*Mein Gott!*" Bauer said for the second time, looking around, as a welcoming entourage of bearded men appeared from a hut, dressed in shirtsleeves, breath steaming in the polar air.

Three

It was a massive underground complex below the Chancellery, bursting with eight hundred people—typists, cooks, chauffeurs, secretaries, orderlies, aides, and advisors. Constructed to last centuries, it contained toilets, running water, small apartments, offices, dining rooms, and conference halls, all protected by six-foot-thick concrete walls. With pride, Adolf Hitler named it the Fuehrerbunker. Here, Hitler would make his stand with his faithful, living like a party of bats.

Martin Bormann entered his fifteen-square-foot office of cold, grey concrete. Today was his third day in the Fuehrerbunker. He had come off a comfortable night's rest, and had been sleeping soundly since his week-long trip to see his wife Gerda. Beneath a large framed picture of Hitler staring down at him, Bormann began his day by ripping the previous sheet off the day calendar on his desk. He looked around. Things were finally getting organized. Files put away. Boxes unpacked. He hated confusion.

Bormann was content with the layout of the department. He had organized it his way, down to the last detail. He had three doors built in which to come and go. One of the doors opened into Josef Goebbels's office, now empty, but soon to be occupied. That was perfect for Bormann. He'd keep an eye on the propaganda minister, the little mole, so he couldn't get too close to Hitler. The second door opened onto the telephone exchange and communications centre, where Bormann could carefully screen all the messages to and from the bunker. The third door led to the conference room where all of Hitler's meetings—arranged by

27

none other than Bormann—took place. Hitler's nearby private bunker contained eighteen rooms, complete with his own telephone exchange, powerhouse, washrooms, and a separate room for his dog, Blondi, and her pup, Wolf. Here, underground, Hitler once again was content to let Bormann deal with the people.

Bormann leafed through the paperwork on his desk. Next door the powerhouse diesel engine, which supplied the ventilation and electrical systems for the entire bunker, banged away, a constant clatter that Bormann forced himself to get used to. Too bad nothing could be done about the stale air.

Bormann looked up. His secretary, a member of his staff for three years, stood at the door. He smiled. "Good morning, Fraulein Krueger."

"Good morning, Herr Reichsleiter." The pretty, thirty-year-old Else Krueger was a professional, all utterly business with her superior. "I have a message for you from Reichmarshall Goering. He will be arriving at the Fuehrerbunker at two this afternoon to see the Fuehrer."

"Thank you, Fraulein Krueger." Bormann smiled. *Ah, Herr Meier.*

"You are welcome."

"Anything else?"

"No, Herr Reichsleiter. That is all."

She turned to leave. Bormann watched her. She was the one woman on his staff whom he hadn't fondled at work or slept with at night, because he knew she was one who wouldn't put up with such advances. For that he actually respected his secretary. She was one of only three women he regarded graciously. The other two were Gerda and his mistress, the actress Manja Behrens, whom he had spent a night with on his way back to Berlin after the week with Gerda.

The two superbly-uniformed men walked in the Chancellery garden, above the bunker, away from sentries patrolling the entrance.

Reichmarshall Hermann Goering was a flag without a pole. Hitler's official successor since 1940, Goering was a leader on paper only of an air force that barely existed except for a few airplanes and a handful of untrained pilots. Tired, shaky, considerably thinner in the last year or so, he was an old fifty-two, a heavy drinker, and a drug addict. He was in the Fuehrer's doghouse since the Luftwaffe had lost the Battle of Britain in 1940. And it never got better after that. Following a poor showing on the Russian Front in 1942 and 1943, Hitler wanted to hang Goering along with his entire Luftwaffe of fliers.

The Reichsmarshall looked distraught during the walk with Bormann. Once the epitome of the socially prominent, once reckless, loud, egotistical, brutal, and extremely obese, Goering was only a crust of a man now with a bad hip that had bothered him since the Great War. "May God have mercy on our souls," he had told Hitler when war broke out six years ago, when Germany was riding high. The war's effects had carved yet more jagged lines in his placid face. He knew he never should have said what he did to the German press in 1939. "Not a single bomb will fall on the Ruhr. If an enemy plane reaches the Ruhr, my name is not Hermann Goering. You can call me Meier!" RAF bombers had not only reached and bombed the Ruhr repeatedly in the last three years, but they had razed Berlin too. Now, in early 1945, only one thing remained constant. Herr Meier still insisted on wearing his lavish, comical uniforms, as was the case today with his white battle dress full of shiny medals under his open greatcoat.

Bormann listened impatiently to Goering's complaints of his sore hip and sorry state of the Luftwaffe and the war before he finally spoke out of desperation to the Reichsmarshall. "Our only hope is that crazy fighter-interceptor of yours, the V-4."

"The V-4?"

"Yes. What the Allied papers call the Foo Fighter."

Goering came to an abrupt stop by the garden wall, scarred and damaged by the winter Allied bombing. "What are you talking about?" he blinked in disbelief, his breath steaming in the cool air.

"The latest secret weapon. I know the codename. *Projekt Equinox*. The combined effort of Messerschmitt and the Peenemunde staff. Isn't that what you came to speak to the Fuehrer about?"

Goering swallowed, unable to speak. His hands, clutching his Reichsmarshall baton, twitched slightly as he stood.

"You can't hide it from me," Bormann continued. "I have pictures in my safe taken inside the underground factory in the Thuringia mountains." Bormann did up another button on his coat to keep the cold out. "They show the radio-controlled models. Your operational tests, I've heard, have been quite successful. Your interceptors have shot down American and British bombers in the last two days. And

29

what is this new pilot-controlled prototype at Peenemunde? I am also familiar with Camp Berlin. So there!"

"Then you do—" Goering stood open-jawed, drawing back a step.

"Close your damn mouth and listen to me, you fool."

"How dare you!"

"We need each other, Goering. The war is as good as over. A blind man can see it."

"That can't be any more apparent. A quick end to the war is inevitable," Goering admitted. "It's only months away. April or May, the latest."

"Then we agree."

"Yes, of course."

"We have to get out of this mess. That's why we created our fraternity in the first place. Certain people will want our technology. *Americans.* May I suggest a solution?"

"I'm listening."

"You and me, Goering, our safety in another country, in exchange for the blueprints to every Nazi secret weapon, except the V-4."

"Why not the V-4? I thought you just said it was our only hope."

"We hold it in reserve, to see if they negotiate without it. We give them the window dressing first. We spring the V-4 on them at the last minute, only if we have to. The less people see it, the better. Are you with me?"

"You and me? An odd combination, wouldn't you say, after all these years?"

Bormann knew what Goering was driving at. They had never come remotely close to being friends. Without question, they had loathed each other. Bormann would now go to work on the Reich Marshall's Achilles heel—his pride. "That was the past. Yes, Goering. You and me. No one else. Not Himmler. Not Goebbels. Not the Fuehrer. They are not members of the Order. Not anyone else. Too many cooks spoil the broth. I can't trust anyone else. We—you and I—see things in a brighter light. We are the only two with a clear sense of self-preservation."

"Then you need me, Bormann?" Goering asserted, with contempt. "You actually trust me. Isn't that lovely. A peaceful coexistence within the High Command."

"Yes. A common course. Let's resolve our differences. Forget the past. Haven't I done so by creating our Order?"

"I have the copies of the original blueprints. I can negotiate myself. Why do I need you?" Goering said, testing Bormann.

"I thought you might say that. Yes, indeed, you may have the Luftwaffe inventions. But I have my Swiss connections."

"So do I. All of us in the High Command do."

"But my banker in Zurich knows Allen Dulles of the OSS quite well."

"The hell you say? Dulles?"

"It's true. The same Allen Dulles who would like nothing better than an Allied-Nazi alliance to fend off the Russians. The same Dulles who gave us the Russian plans for Europe."

"How do you know this?"

"Believe me, I know it. Everything the Fuehrer knows, I know. Dulles was also at one time the legal advisor to the Anglo-German Schroeder Bank, before he became the OSS Director in Switzerland."

"The Schroeder Bank?"

"Yes."

"I.S. Filberg's bank?"

"That is correct, yes. Our own German industrial cartel, I.S. Filberg, who went begging, hat in hand, to Wall Street to finance our National Socialist movement in the first place. And remember, it was a Schroeder group that merged with a Rockefeller group before the war to become the Schroeder Rockefeller Company. Our American connection may come through for us once again, when we need them most."

"Can you vouch for your banker?"

"Yes, of course I can."

"Even so, how do you know the OSS will wish to deal with us?"

"Oh, they will. They'd be fools not to. We have too much on Dulles and other Americans who've been secretly supplying us with oil and aluminium since the war began."

Goering twirled his baton, resting it by his right leg. "How can you be sure it will work out as you say? How badly do the Americans want our inventions?"

"Basic greed on their part. They don't want the Russians to get what we have. In addition, my banker is, allow me to say, persuasive."

"Let me think this through. I'll get back to you."

"Don't take too long. Let me stress the reality that our world is getting smaller every day. The Allies are seeing to it."

"Do you think I don't know that?" Goering huffed.

They walked to the gate leading out to the rubbled street. Together, they raised their right hand in the Nazi salute, then placed the same hand to their heart. . . a pledge of support as clandestine brothers in the second degree of the Order of the Knights of National Socialism.

"Blood brother, Herr Bormann."

It was quite comical to the Reichsleiter, who knew that each one was out to bleed whatever they could from the arrangement. "Blood brother, Herr Goering."

"Good day, Bormann," Goering said, his face hard.

Bormann watched Goering leave by way of the pot-holed street to his limousine across the road. The secret fraternity initiated by Bormann in August, 1944 was starting to pay off. After the Allied D-Day landing in early June of that year, Bormann was quick to predict that the end was very near. Pulling his old adversary, Herr Meier, into the group was a strategic move. The V-4 was under Goering's umbrella. Bormann needed the nervous wreck of a man. For the present. The trap had been laid. Goering was a bigger idiot than Bormann first thought.

Bormann saw that there were many possible places in which to hide out in the next few months. Argentina. Neuschwabenland. America. He only had to take his pick.

For the present, back to Adolf the Great. His drugs. His steady stream of chocolates. And his tantrums.

SOUTHERN ENGLAND

Cloudy weather over the continent had grounded the operation for three days. But not tonight. Clear skies were expected.

The fighter pilot flicked the mike switch to the side of his oxygen mask to "on."

"SILVER SIX-THREE TO EMERALD TOWER. OK TO TAKE-OFF?"

"EMERALD TOWER TO SILVER SIX-THREE, YOU ARE CLEARED TO TAKE-OFF. GOOD HUNTING."

The pilot pushed the dual throttles to maximum, watching the revolutions climb on the brightly-lit panel at eye-level. Twenty-five hundred horsepower from his twin Merlin engines roared in his ears.

He released the brakes.

A kick in the pants. . . and they were off in the twilight. The pilot glanced right to his navigator in the seat tucked against his, then lifted the Mosquito fighter off the runway. He brought the landing gear up and banked the machine east.

In minutes, Bevens and Solomon were over the North Sea, heading towards Germany. As a night intruder, their mission was to check out and aggravate one of the last fighter bases in Germany—near Hamburg—that was still harassing the Royal Air Force bombers on their nightly raids of the Fatherland. And it had to be done—again—before the bombers came over tonight on a raid to Berlin.

Part-way over the North Sea, the pilot released the fifty-gallon drop tanks and went to the wing tanks. Night had fallen. They climbed to 2,500 feet. He could hear a buzzing in his headset. Enemy scanners were already on them.

With a small flashlight, British navigator Bill Bevens studied the maps on his knees. He glanced up. According to his calculations via his panel equipment, the checkpoint should be coming up in six minutes.

"TURN PORT THREE DEGREES," he said into his mask to Canadian pilot, Reggie Solomon. Masks on, complete with the earphones, was the best form of communication with the constant roar of the engines around them.

"YOU BET."

"CHECKPOINT IN TWO MINUTES, TWENTY SECONDS."

"ROGER."

Solomon nosed the fighter down to the water line. He would be coming under the coastal radar at zero altitude, north of Bremerhaven. The German coast came up quickly. . . and flashed beneath. Then he brought the stick back, sending the fighter into a stiff climb. At 2,000 feet, he levelled off, then turned southeast on his navigator's directions.

HAMBURG

The supervisor attached to Zerstorer Unit 22 peered over the shoulder of his radar technician inside the darkened room. The two watched the pulsing, green blip and the green wide-sweeping arm on the screen.

"There it is, Herr Leyberger," the technician said, recording the time with a pencil in his log. "In our sector. By that speed and the size of the target, I would have to say it's none other than an intruder Mosquito."

The supervisor smiled, bending over the glowing machine. "Let's give him a little surprise. I will alert Loebitz. A single interceptor should be sufficient."

"I agree, Herr Leyberger. One on one."

"Yes, it will be rather *sporting*."

Northern Germany

A winding river, attached to a tear-drop shaped piece of water glistened at them in the moonlight. "THERE'S THE LAKE," Bevens said.

"GOT IT."

"TURN FIVE DEGREES STARBOARD. WE SHOULD BE OVER DAAKAN FAIRLY SOON."

It took two minutes to see landing lights. Solomon banked left in a tight circle, nose down.

"WE GOT ONE COMING IN TO LAND."

Solomon nodded. His navigator was right. What appeared to be an ME-109 was in the circuit and approaching the downwind leg. Solomon flicked his gun safety switch to the firing position and gave chase. Solomon raced across the field and caught the German fighter from the side with a burst of fire. Whether he connected or not, he'd never know. He kept his finger on the button, aiming for the other fighters on the dispersal track.

He hit one and it exploded into flames. Then Daakan airfield plunged into darkness. A searchlight beam blinked on. Solomon banked low over the base, turned, and fired at the light. It went out. Solomon climbed and headed west. Mission accomplished.

Then. . . a flash of light flew by overhead, heading in the opposite direction.

"WHAT WAS THAT?"

"DON'T KNOW. A FALLING STAR, MAYBE."

"I DON'T THINK SO."

Banking the Mosquito to starboard, Solomon and his navigator both watched a glowing orange light streak off at a tremendous speed.

"I SAY, LOOK AT THAT BUGGER GO!"

"WAIT. . . IT'S TURNING."

Solomon looked over his shoulder. It was no falling star. It had to be man-made.

"WHATEVER IT IS, IT KNOWS WE'RE HERE." Solomon advanced the throttles to a healthy four hundred miles per hour.

It was not enough.

The light came up from behind and overtook the Mosquito in seconds, then raced ahead of them as if they were standing in mid-air. Solomon took a few shots at it, and missed. It was much too quick.

"WHAT THE—" Solomon gulped into his mask. He had always thought the Mosquito to be the fastest fighter in both air forces, British and German. Not so. Was this thing a fighter? Of course it was a fighter. What else was it? Maybe it was one of those German jets. But even the jets couldn't be this fast.

Solomon banked to port, the direction of home.

England.

The light appeared out of nowhere and headed right for them. Nose to nose! From a hundred yards away, it flew straight up and disappeared into a layer of clouds, turning the sky above them a dusty orange.

Solomon never let up on the throttles.

"HERE IT COMES AGAIN!" the navigator warned, glancing over his shoulder at the light falling out of the clouds in a tight U-turn. "HEAD FOR THE DECK!"

It was on their tail in a flash. A hundred yards back, it slowed down. . . then sped up, letting loose a spray at the Mosquito's engine exhaust, before darting straight up into the clouds again.

The British fighter disintegrated, spreading molten debris over enemy territory. Bevens and Solomon died instantly.

HAMBURG

The technician watched with childlike excitement as the unidentified blip disappeared off the radar screen, leaving only the wide, pulsing, green sweep.

"It's gone, Herr Leyberger," he sighed, hiding a grin. "I take it to mean one thing."

The supervisor walked over. "I know. For them the war is over. I will return the interceptor to base. Well done, Wolfgang."

"Thank you, Herr Leyberger. I wish I was there to see it."

"Me, too."

Four

Otto Bauer savoured a swig of hot, strong coffee from his glass mug inside the wooden hut, as he and a younger associate studied the lead samples brought to them off the ridge.

"Still too low grade," Bauer sighed, magnifying glass to his eye. He scratched his beard, now nearly as full as the others in the camp.

"But it is improving in quality as we drill deeper in the rock."

Bauer agreed, sniffing. He was fighting off a cold. "What depth are we now?"

"One hundred meters."

"We have to go even deeper, or else go farther inland and start all over again."

"Where there's more ice to drill through?" the associate asked. "I don't expect Wilhelm to agree to that."

"No, I suppose not." Bauer swallowed more coffee, grunting, sniffing, wiping his nose with a handkerchief. Two weeks and barely anything worthwhile removed from the ground. He had to be patient. *Do your duty*, he remembered.

The phone rang.

"Otto, it's for you," said a third man inside the hut.

The scientist walked over to the desk phone opposite the dirty window. "Hello."

"Otto, it's Wilhelm."

"Yes, Wilhelm," Bauer replied. "I hope *you* have some good news, better than the samples so far."

37

"I do." Wilhelm Raeder sounded excited. "Our number two search squad reported in."

"Where have they been? We haven't heard from them for two days."

"Radio malfunction, and a bad storm inland, so they said. Nevertheless, they found something worthwhile."

"And what did they find?"

"Won't you be surprised?"

"I'm beginning to think that I will. Are you going to keep me in suspense?"

"Get dressed. Warm. We are going on a journey. Be ready in five minutes," Raeder ordered, with a voice of authority.

The journey was slow over the dry snow. The wind blew, but not hard enough to hamper visibility to any great degree. Raeder drove, navigating by a large compass and radio communication with his search team. After a slow thirty kilometres into the interior, Raeder slammed on the brakes of the canvas-covered jeep beside another covered jeep. They were in a wide, flat clearing several kilometres across.

The driver rolled down his window and gestured towards a rise to the right. "Another kilometre or more. That way."

"Right."

They lumbered on until the driver drew his vehicle to a halt. "Here it is," the driver said, proudly.

Bauer stepped out onto mushy, wet snow and gazed upon a steaming pool of water approximately ten feet by fifteen feet. He bent down. The pool was clear, rocks at the bottom. The air over it warm, almost hot. He wiped his nose.

Reader followed behind. "Hot springs."

"I can see that." Bauer shook his head, sniffing. "Unbelievable."

"Yes, isn't it. In the Antarctic."

"No, I mean, you brought me all the way out here to show me some damn hot springs?"

Raeder smiled. "Yes and no." The geologist went to the rear of the jeep, threw off the canvas cover, and returned with four crystal glasses and the bottle of wine that Bauer had brought from Germany. "Otto, I learned a long time ago that one must always keep a sense of humour in addition to a sense of reality. With that in mind, we celebrate."

"Why?" Bauer replied, confused.

"Time to break open Wernher's French wine. Boys, jump in. You too, Otto. Might do wonders for your cold and your mood."

"I hope to hell it does."

They all stripped naked, threw their heavy clothes on the warm rocks and eased into the hot water, which had to be over a hundred degrees. Soon they were squatting in a pool up to their chests.

Raeder poured the wine. "A toast. . . to our luck."

They clinked glasses, and drank.

"What luck is that?" Bauer asked, licking his lips, the dark, red wine stinging his throat. The combination of steamy water and powerful wine was actually clearing his sinuses. "Excellent, I must admit."

"Don't you see?" Raeder answered. "This must have been a volcanic region at one time, thousands or millions of years ago. I wonder what's under all this ice?"

"Or perhaps," Bauer interrupted, thinking of what the sub skipper had said about the trip under the continent, "it still is volcanic. Far beneath the earth. Oftentimes, cold areas can have the hottest springs. Iceland, for example."

"Greenland, too," Raeder agreed. "I saw them. I was there in 1939 and 1941, before the Americans forced us out and built their air bases." Raeder dunked his head under the water, then popped up, massaging his hand through his slicked hair. "Otto, as a geologist I know that where there's hot springs, there's minerals. Sometimes close to the surface. We might be on to something. We're going to have to move our drilling team. Right here."

Bauer pondered Raeder's assumption, staring into the wine. "Now I see."

"Drink up, my friend!" Raeder laughed. "Drink up!"

"I just might do that."

LONDON

Alone in the projection room, Wesley Hollinger read the OSS dispatches—intercepted radio signals—brought to his attention. Obviously the Germans had added something to their already-potent arsenal. Loebitz airfield had a new fighter and were in direct communication with Hamburg. New call signs and codenames had been exercised.

But, strange. . . no radio communication with the pilots, or at least not recorded. Very bizarre.

Hollinger tossed the dispatches on the seat next to him. He stood up to press the button on the side of the projector to start the film that he would see for the first time, a short piece that had been smuggled out of Germany. He shut the room light off and let the film roll. The footage was amazingly clear, with sound, and in colour! No need to act surprised. The Germans were highly advanced in such technology. Hollinger immediately recognized the rocket-powered Messerschmitt ME-163 Komet, one of the most radical and futuristic of German aerial designs. Single-seated and single-engined. According to sources, it was capable of reaching the speed of sound in level flight. The ME-163 was a short fighter, Hollinger could tell right off by the pilot standing beside it. It was also quite ugly, like a lop-sided torpedo. But looks meant nothing to the American agent once he saw the aircraft take off down the grass strip on its jettisoned trolley at a fantastic speed, smoke belching from its exhaust. It then climbed nearly straight up to the clouds. . . in seconds!

Hollinger gaped at the screen. Dorwin was right about one thing in his assessment of the situation in Germany. The Germans were years ahead of the Allies in aeronautical research.

What else did they have?

Werra, Germany

Heinrich Himmler strutted alongside the fighter production line, the nervous SS commandant in charge of the underground facility closely at his heels like an obedient puppy, eager to please. In the midst of the noise of construction—banging, drilling, shouts from supervisors—the commandant methodically explained the work at each station.

Together they viewed the initial stages of the strange wing formation, the landing gear, the armament, and the centre section of the Messerschmitt V-4 Experimental Series 1-1a fighter-interceptor. Following the line, they saw how the pieces were sent on rails to the next area where they were riveted in place. The rest, up the line, were finishing touches. The Reichsfuehrer and the commandant walked to the end and out the mountain tunnel entrance guarded by six tall SS guards. Outside, another SS guard was beating a skinny, pale man with a whip.

"Does this happen often, Herr Colonel?" Himmler's tone was matter-of-fact.

The commandant, Colonel Geinns, swallowed hard and stared at the man in the sinister black uniform and high polished boots. "The beatings?"

"Yes, the beatings. What did you think I meant?"

"Yes. . . well. . . sometimes we do have to. . . discipline our workers, Herr Reichsfuehrer. We have to. However, conditions—"

"You had an escape last month. One of the Polish prisoners."

The commandant tried to explain. "Yes, true, but—"

"The Fuehrer has placed a high priority on *Projekt Equinox*. Let me remind you, Herr Colonel, this is a top-secret installation. There will be no other escapes."

"Yes, of course, Herr Reichsfuehrer. But we caught the prisoner in thirty minutes. Since then, we have beefed up the lighting outside the entrance and have constructed a much higher wire fence." He sighed. "However, I must point out that the conditions are not the best here, Herr Reichsfuehrer."

"What do you mean?"

"Our food supply for the prisoners is decreasing," the commandant explained. "Fresh water is scarce. Very few supplies are getting through, even to the guards. Word is that our trains are being shot up enroute by Allied fighters. We cannot go on like this."

"You're not the only one. . . feeling the pressure. We must all make sacrifices at this time for the Fuehrer and the Fatherland."

The commandant turned away for a moment to watch the guard whip and kick the worker into the tunnel, as the other guards chuckled with laughter. "Yes, of course, Herr Reichsfuehrer."

"Stop that prisoner!" Himmler demanded.

From forty feet away, the commandant deftly passed the order to the guard, who swung the prisoner around by the scruff of his neck.

"What do you want with him, Herr Reichsfuchrer?" the commandant asked.

"What did he do to deserve the beating?"

"What did he do?" the commandant called out to the guard.

"He was caught sleeping on the line, Herr Colonel," the guard answered.

Himmler sighed. "Shoot him."

"Herr Reichsfuehrer?"

"I said shoot him! Now! Are you deaf? You must set an example for the others."

"Shoot him!" the commandant ordered the guard.

The SS guard's reaction was instantaneous. He grabbed the terrified prisoner by his coat and dragged him into the open.

"No! No!" the prisoner shouted, falling to his knees. "Please, no!"

Himmler turned from the entrance and walked away with the colonel. "These. . . flying tops are wreaking havoc on the enemy bombers are they?"

The commandant cleared the bile in his throat. "Yes, they are, Herr Reichsfuehrer. I am told so by the Luftwaffe High Command."

Himmler nodded, approvingly. "Do you believe the Third Reich will win the war, Herr Colonel?"

"Certainly, Herr Reichsfuehrer. No one will conquer the German spirit."

Himmler slipped the commandant an uneasy glance, as two pistol shots rang out behind them. "It would be wise to quit your complaining. Loyalty, unconditional loyalty, is the true quality of a man. The highest of duties."

"Yes, Herr Reichsfuehrer."

"Nonetheless, your men have performed well, and so have you, despite the escape."

"You are too kind, Herr Reichsfuehrer."

"Yes, I am. Goodbye, Colonel Geinns. Heil Hitler."

"Heil Hitler!" The commandant saluted smartly, snatching a quick glance over to the dead prisoner lying on the ground, shot through the head.

Himmler spun on his heels and moved off to his waiting limousine.

On the airplane, returning to his command post north of Berlin, Heinrich Himmler jotted in his diary, *Projekt Equinox last chance before drastic measures are taken.*

Weary, the Reichsfuehrer closed his eyes, and leaned back into the seat, while the stripped-down Junkers passenger plane continued to climb over the Thuringia Mountains. One of the most powerful men in what was left of the Nazi regime, the Reichsfuehrer was stretched to the limit these dark days. He was the head of the Gestapo state police, and the SS, Hitler's personal guard. He controlled all German domestic and foreign Intelligence and most of the concentration camps. He was the ultimate military power in the northern German zone, Norway, Scandinavia, and Holland, as well as the chief of the Replacement Army and the newly-established Army Group Vistula fighting forces. He was Hitler's perfect *yes-man*. He followed Hitler's orders with no sense of guilt. If the Fuehrer wanted all Germans with surnames beginning with the letter Y be shot, then Himmler would do it. No questions asked. He could give a man dinner one night, laugh and joke with him, then issue a death warrant for him the following morning, with no qualms.

At this time the Nazi regime had no new territory to conquer and imprison people against their will. They hadn't for three years. The Nazis were on the run. The Allies were closing in from all sides. Contrary to what he told the commandant, Himmler knew the war was lost. The situation was in peril. The radio-controlled fighters of *Projekt Equinox* would not win the war. Had they come out earlier, combined with the rest of the secret weapon arsenal, then maybe. Water under the bridge at this stage of the game. And to think his SS could have been the breeding bulls for the future master race of Aryan purity—tall, muscular, blonde-haired, blue-eyed specimens of loyalty and honour who swore an oath before God that they would give absolute allegiance to the Fuehrer and be ready to lay down their life for their master.

No more.

Deep in his own solitude, Himmler considered his options. There weren't many. One and only one came to mind. He would have to seek peace with the West. On his own.

Five

Wesley Hollinger was struck by his president's lethargic physical condition.

Hollinger had heard that Franklin Roosevelt was a sick man. But this bad? He had lost weight. His eyes stared off into space. His mouth drooped to one side. His hands were shaky. His vitality of four years ago had completely disappeared. Dorwin was right again. Roosevelt wasn't himself. Not by any stretch of the imagination. *This man* was running the United States and half the world? At this rate, not for long. He'd be lucky to hang on until spring.

Hollinger stood with the others in the group of newspaperman and film crews that watched the Big Three leaders—Roosevelt, Joe Stalin, and Winston Churchill—pose and answer questions for the eager press outside the Livadia Palace Black Sea resort in the Crimea on this cool February day. A flashbulb popped in Roosevelt's face. He seemed stunned for a moment. Then he turned to Churchill on the right. Hollinger wondered what the two were discussing. How Nazi Germany's spoils would be divided up in the new, soon-to-come, post-war New World Order? What should happen to Hitler, if they caught the monster? What concessions did Stalin want? It would all come to a head in the next few days in a series of eight specific conferences in which Roosevelt was expected to be the mediator between Stalin and Churchill.

To Hollinger, Churchill hadn't appeared any different since the last meeting, just a little older. Still full of spark, though. Stalin was another matter. This was Hollinger's first glimpse of the mighty Soviet dictator whose armies were crushing the Germans in the east. Never without a cigarette, Stalin was quite short, less than five and a half feet tall, with a distinct, thick moustache. The dictator was taking it all in. At one point he smiled graciously for the cameras. But Hollinger saw something sinister behind his sleepy "Uncle Joe" manner. The other two leaders had come to his territory to satisfy him. Hollinger knew that much from sources. Just how much was Joe going to get away with?

Time would tell.

Alone with the president that evening in his furnished room, Hollinger took a glass of vodka handed him and drank a small mouthful. Up close, under the lights, Roosevelt looked worse than he did in the resort garden, taking on the appearance of a true invalid in his wheelchair.

"Sit down, Wesley," the president uttered, sighing. "It's been awhile." His hands were folded in his lap, his eyes glassy. On doctor's orders, he wasn't drinking.

Hollinger eased into a padded, beige sofa, his fedora by his side. Outside, a misty rain began to let up just as night drifted over the Crimea. "Yes, sir, it has been some time."

"The summer of 1941. You were filling me in on that oddball Rudolf Hess case in the Oval Office."

"That's right, sir, I was."

The president stared at the wall, silent for many moments. Then he manufactured a ghostly, pathetic smile. "I seem to recall also that I saw you in the balcony at the House of Representatives. I was giving a speech that day. Now, what was it for?"

Hollinger felt sorry for his commander in chief for not remembering such an important event. "The day after Pearl Harbor, sir. You had asked Congress to declare a state of war against the Empire of Japan."

"Oh, yes." Roosevelt nodded slowly. "How could I forget? I've been doing that lately. Forgetting things." He turned away.

They both felt the long, lead-weight silence between them.

"Wesley, I summoned you here because I know you'd give me straight answers as always."

"I'll try, sir." When the next silence was too long, Hollinger asked, "What exactly did you want to ask me?"

"It's this Nazi technology."

Hollinger braced himself. "What about it?"

"Donovan tells me your OSS department is investigating and filing such material for the future. After the war, I hear."

The agent recalled Dorwin's warning. SI and OSS first. "You heard right, sir. That's true, we are. The United States can make use of all their inventions. The V-1s and V-2s. The jet fighters."

"The Soviets want everything to be shared with them."

"Do they now?"

"What do you think?"

"Is this room bugged?"

The president grinned, slowly. "No. It was checked out by our people the minute we arrived."

"Do you want my honest opinion?"

"Yes. Straight answers. Remember?"

"OK, sir. Piss on them. Pardon my Russian. I wouldn't trust those buggers as far as I can throw them," Hollinger said. "I mean that in all honesty."

"That so?"

"And I think that we'd sure as hell better get to these launch sites and factories before Uncle Joe does. Because if he beats us to the punch, he won't share a damn thing with us."

"Churchill has been telling me the same thing."

Then listen to him, thought Hollinger. "Churchill's a good man."

"What exactly do you have? Pictures? Blueprints?"

Wesley knew he had to lie here. He stared squarely at the president. "Only stories and some smuggled out photos, so far."

"What about this new secret fighter?"

"You must mean the 262?"

"No."

"The rocket—the Komet?"

"No. There's rumours of something else out there over the European skies, so Stalin tells me. The latest Nazi weapon."

"Nothing like this has been brought to my attention. Not yet."

The president thought long and hard. "I see. Who's the German authority behind all these missiles and strange things? What's his name?"

"Wernher von Braun, sir."

"Yes, he's the one. Extraordinary man. A genius, I hear."

"So they say. We could use him on our side. We want him."

"For sure. Have you made contact with him?"

"No, sir. He is too closely guarded by Luftwaffe and Gestapo Intelligence."

"You know, there's more at stake than just Nazi secret weapons. There's bigger forces at work."

"How do you mean, sir?"

"Bigger than me, that's what."

"Who are you referring to, sir?"

"One of these days, maybe in your lifetime, all countries will unite. A new world government is coming. One day you might see it laid out before you. Compromise, that's what I have to do in this changing planet of ours. What every politician has to do. Oh, never mind. You get tired of it after a while."

"I'm sure you do, sir. And I'm sure that Stalin wants more than meets the eye."

The president seemed to deflate. "We suspect he'll want some American loans to reconstruct."

Hollinger grunted. "I knew it. After all that he received in Lend-Lease. He has the gall. It should be a two-way street. What's he about to give up?"

"We have to force him to conduct free elections in all the countries he has annexed in his march east."

"Fat chance of that, sir." Hollinger sipped at his vodka.

Roosevelt turned his wheelchair around, and creaked across the Persian rug, towards the window. "That's why I like you, Wesley. It's your honesty," he said, his back to the agent.

"You asked me for straight answers, Mr. President."

"Yes, and I got them. I respect that."

After another long silence, Hollinger asked, "Sir, what are we going to get out of this conference? What's in it for us?"

"We have to secure an agreement with the Russians about a new United Nations organization, where all countries will benefit. Germany will be divided into four occupation zones. Us, the British, the Russians, and the French. I came here as a referee. I believe the only difference between us, the British, and the Russians, is just a matter of words."

"In my opinion, sir, I see a new and wicked world coming. Worse than we've seen in the last six years. Give those Russian bastards too much, and we'll live to regret it."

The president turned around, brooding and poised. "This is where we disagree, Wesley."

"Yes, sir, I suppose it is then."

"Nevertheless, I appreciate you coming and giving it to me straight. I won't detain you any longer. Go and enjoy yourself."

Hollinger set his empty glass down on a table, and drew himself upright to his feet, grabbing his fedora. "I wish it would warm up. Isn't it usually balmy here?" And where were Dorwin's bathing beauties?

"Just a cool spell. It still beats Washington," the leader said. "I'll see you out."

"Thank you, Mr. President."

When Hollinger left in a hurry, and closed the door behind him, he came to one clear conclusion. Contrary to the earlier Casablanca and Tehran conferences, Roosevelt had come to Yalta with no prepared American agenda except to suck up to Stalin at any price.

What gives?

Six

The technician removed the fourteen-inch-long wooden model from the metal case and placed it inside the long chamber. The Area 14 supersonic wind-tunnel test, capable of simulating 4000 miles per hour, would tell all. They hoped.

Two scientists in white smocks stood beside the thick panes of plate glass next to the test room. The technician emerged from the chamber, and trotted to the corner by the door and placed his hand on a switch on his board instrumentation.

"How does Goering expect us to operate under such conditions," Karl Zeller whispered to his friend, Wernher von Braun, the brains behind Peenemunde. "Dwindling funds. Under heavy guard twenty-four hours a day."

"Hush! Not so loud."

They exchanged glances. Together, the two scientists shared the same common ground, a disdain for their country's leaders and Nazi government meddling. Not to mention the Luftwaffe in the compound, the SS in the neighbouring V-2 facility and Gestapo always poking around outside.

"Sorry, Wernher."

"We shall overcome. The future, Karl. Remember the future. This regime will perish before the summer heat descends on us."

"But will we be alive to revel in its demise?"

"Be optimistic," von Braun advised him.

"I'm trying to be."

"Are you ready?" von Braun raised his voice, gesturing to the technician.

"Yes."

"Then begin."

The technician pressed the switch. A valve opened, forcing outside air into several large funnels. Then the air was rammed through drying filters, and finally transferred to sheet-metal straighteners inside the tunnel. A sound began—a slow, steady moan, deep within the bowels of the chamber. Then it grew louder and higher pitched. The airflow smoothed out, then raced to supersonic speed.

Zeller joined the technician at the controls. "Mach one," Zeller said, reading the instruments.

Von Braun nodded, his face hard, his arms folded. It was a perfect parallel flow of air over the suspended aircraft model.

"Mach one-point-two."

Von Braun waved to increase speed. "More!"

"Mach one-point-five."

Von Braun's eyes were fixed to the wing surface nearest the bubble cockpit. No restrictions. The white airflow steady. Everything functioning.

"Mach one-point-eight!"

Von Braun checked his watch as speeds soared above Mach two.

Twenty seconds was always the limit. No more. Time was up. He turned to the technician, and yelled, "Cut it!"

The scream died down, slowly, then fell silent.

"That's fine. Leave us."

"Yes, Herr Doctor."

The technician withdrew and closed the door behind him.

"It works, Wernher."

"Yes. Excellent. Come sit down, Karl. Relax. You've been working too hard."

The wind-tunnel room inside Haus 12 was one of the few places where the Director of Peenemunde Army Weapons Department, thirty-two-year-old Wernher von Braun, could talk to his friend and associate at the Luftwaffe Experimental Station on the Baltic coast island. They were surrounded by an airfield with hangars, laboratories, test stands, air-raid shelters, all part of a far-reaching operation at Peenemunde where 2,000 engineers and scientists were housed, along with 4,000 support staff. Guards were everywhere, on orders from Berlin. In the next compound the V-2 intercontinental rocket had been tested, the same rocket that had rained destruction at four times the speed of sound on the terrified Allied cities of Paris and London.

The pace at Peenemunde was fast and intense. *Work, work, work. Tests, tests, tests.* Meetings every day. Sixty-to-eighty hour workweeks were the norm. Tired men often slept on cots between tests. In the summer, for relaxation, the staff would swim off the beaches that were only five hundred yards away or take a casual bicycle trip over the island. Von Braun, a bachelor, chose to play his cello in off-hours, or navigate his sailboat about the island, often with a woman or women aboard. Handsome, confident, wavy-haired von Braun was the rocket genius that Berlin was counting on to lead Germany to ultimate victory with the secret weapons that Hitler had promised his people. Von Braun was a tidy, elegant man, graceful, proud, self-assured. Together with Zeller and the others, von Braun and the Peenemunde team had seen their way through the other projects, including the V-2. Now the V-4 in conjunction with the Messerschmitt factory was the latest of the toys. All under pressure from Berlin to produce. . . and in a hurry. In his years of research, he had seen more politics than he had thought possible. And it wasn't getting any better.

The younger Zeller sat down with von Braun. Not yet thirty, Zeller had been by his friend's side since 1941, one of the first to join the talented Peenemunde team. He was fair-skinned and owned a knot of black, curly hair. Like von Braun, his background in government-funded rocket research dated back to the 1930s.

"Is it safe to speak, Wernher?"

"Here? Oh, yes."

"How much longer will this unnecessary killing continue, Wernher?"

"Only a short time. We cannot lose faith in ourselves. We must not! Space travel, that's what all this will lead to. The moon. The planets. We are among the pioneers. And you are one of my brightest stars. I need you. We must remain unscathed to share the information with the world."

If the compliment pleased Zeller, he didn't show it. "That's fine if the Americans or British find us first. But the Russians? What about them?"

"We will have to stay out of their way."

"Mein Gott! Easier said than done."

"Let's change the subject, Karl?"

"Why do you avoid discussing the Russians?"

"Because, Karl, what we often fear the most never happens."

No one spoke for several seconds.

"Are you happy with the V-4 test results?"

"That's better, Karl. Indeed, aerodynamically it does have promise. In a lab. But unless those lightweight materials we are looking for are found, the *Projekt Equinox* V-4 pilot version will never obtain such speeds. It was fine as a radio-controlled model. Now Goering wants an undercarriage, with manual and automatic overrides, on-board computers. There's simply no time."

"How is the testing on the new turbojet engine coming along?"

"Slow, at best," von Braun admitted. "I can't see it being ready for, oh, at least three to six months."

"Three to six months!"

"Yes. I heard today. It's the compressor. It can't seem to force enough air into the combustion chambers to ignite the fuel. It's burning too rich by the time it reaches the tail end."

"Herr Goering won't be pleased."

Von Braun stared at Zeller. "He never is. You let me worry about the Reichmarshall. You have enough trouble on your hands with Himmler." Von Braun moved closer. "I wish to suggest in the strongest terms that you watch yourself, my friend, for you are playing a very dangerous game with a very dangerous person. We know what he's capable of. Others have paid a high price for such action as yours. Be careful, should Herr Himmler discover your true motives."

"He won't. He, too, has enough to worry about. His own neck is in a noose."

Von Braun thought hard about that, then smiled. "So right."

"By the way, Wernher, I received a letter from my wife. She is safely in Switzerland. The bombing of Dresden was a perfect screen for her to slip away. After the raid the authorities filed her as one of the thousands who died. She said she will wait for me in Zurich."

"Excellent. I am happy for you both. But you don't look pleased about it. What's wrong?"

"Wernher, I have the strangest of feelings that I will never see her again."

Von Braun pointed his finger at his friend. "Don't think that way."

LONDON

Roberta saw her husband arrive by taxi down below. She closed the curtain, and as the auto roared away she walked quietly across the floor and shocked her husband by whipping the door open before he even had a chance to turn the handle. Then she flew into his arms. He dropped his suitcase to the wood floor.

"Hello yourself," he grinned.

They embraced and their lips collided inside the entrance. They were reunited after two weeks apart.

"Hey, now I like that," Hollinger gasped, breaking off from her.

"I missed you." She stood back. "You put on some weight."

He sucked in his stomach. "The Russian good life. Fatty foods. And you're certainly getting bigger."

She patted her mid-section. "Good grief, I'm bloated, that's what I am. I'm a sow."

"I think you're beautiful."

"Thank you. I like your tan. Did you get any work done at all?"

"Yeah. And I met the man." He pushed the door closed. "He's awful. No. Pathetic is the word."

"Who?"

"President Roosevelt, that's who. He's one sick daddy." He flung his hat on the couch. "I got you some presents." He dug into his suitcase and removed a flat can, a bottle, and a small painting.

She read the side of the can. "Caviar!"

"That's right. And some vodka, and. . ."

"An icon! A Russian icon."

"Do you like it?"

"It's wonderful." She handled the religious image painted on a five-by-seven-inch wood panel.

"Got a drink? I'm parched."

"Wine?"

"Anything."

"That's all we've got."

"I'll take it." Wesley Hollinger eased into the nearby chair. He sighed, his fedora still on his head. "He gave everything away. Our whole future. Roosevelt handed Europe to the Russians on a silver platter. Churchill warned me that it might happen. He was right. Yalta was another Munich."

"Churchill's always right," Roberta laughed, bringing a crystal glass three-quarter-filled with red wine. "He told me so."

Hollinger smirked, taking the drink. "Thanks. What did the papers say over here?"

Roberta shrugged. "The Allies will occupy Germany. There will be a new government in Poland. And. . . a new League of Nations will be formed."

"Yeah, the United Nations. Nothing about the Pacific?"

"No. Should there be?"

"I guess not. It's a secret gentlemen's agreement. Stalin promised to declare war on Japan within three months after Germany's surrender, in return for control of the Kuril Islands off northern Japan. Keep that to yourself."

"Of course. My lips are sealed."

"And they're such cute lips too." He drained a mouthful of wine. "So, what's new with you?"

"Lots. We have a. . . well. . . interrogation coming up."

"Excuse me?"

"We have an appointment at MI-6 Headquarters, at nine AM. Sharp."

Hollinger sat up. "*We*?"

"You and me, cowboy."

"I don't take orders from MI-6. I haven't for. . . what. . . three years."

"You will now. Dorwin called me. He said to be there. He's going to be there, too, with Colonel Lampert."

Hollinger made a puzzled face. "Ah, a joint meeting. I smell something."

"So do I."

"What do you think she's about?"

"I don't have even the foggiest."

"You sure?"

"Honest. Hungry, my dear?"

He jolted to his feet. "I'm starved! Let's go out."

Otto Bauer had been asleep on a cot for two hours, dreaming of Germany... *and his young wife. They were at home in Nuremberg. Alone. Late at night, in the summer. He was in bed, waiting for her. She disrobed completely and moved to him, her sleek body caught by the moonlight streaming in the open window. He slid back the sheets for her. She eased in beside him, bent over, and took his hand. He reached out to touch her with his other hand...*

Bauer didn't hear the door open, but he did feel a heavy tap on his shoulder. He awoke thousands of miles from his homeland to see Wilhelm Raeder leaning over, a grin on his face that spread his mouth and thick beard. Bauer would have preferred his wife.

"We did it."

Bauer rubbed his bleary eyes and focused on the far window. It was still daylight. Then again, it was nearly always daylight this close to the South Pole this time of year. "Did what?"

"We found titanium."

Bauer was awake now. He coughed, the last stage of the cold that had lasted weeks. "Titanium!"

Raeder nodded, eyes flashing.

"Has it been confirmed?"

"Our lab reports never lie."

"Where in heaven's name did you find it?" Bauer sat up.

"Not one hundred meters from the hot springs. Forty feet in the rock. Where there's hot springs, there's minerals."

"Yes. You did say that, as I recall. Now what do we do?"

"Tell our friends at Peenemunde."

Bauer rubbed his whole face with both hands. "Won't they be delighted."

"Yes, won't they. I wish I could be there to see their faces."

Seven

Twenty-four hours after the V-4 wind-tunnel test, Karl Zeller reported to Heinrich Himmler's new command post, a large mansion purchased by the SS in 1938 near Prenzlau, fifty miles north of Berlin. The doctor drove his Mercedes past the SS guard at the gate and into the gravel parking lot. At the front door was another SS guard, who checked the doctor's identification, then told him to take the stairs to the right.

Tired, Zeller entered the first office he saw on the first floor and waited in the anteroom. He didn't know what to expect from the Reichsfuehrer today.

The SS leader looked up from his paperwork. "Dr. Zeller, do come in."

Himmler's SS adjutant, Ludwig Hahn, closed the door to the panelled den. Zeller stepped forward. He was now standing before the ruthless man who controlled the lives of millions of Germans. "Heil Hitler!" he saluted. For a moment, the scientist looked off to the side at the framed oil painting of Frederick the Great.

"Heil Hitler," Himmler replied, his expression distant and cold. "On your way to Berlin, again, are we?"

"Yes, Herr Reichsfuehrer."

"Anything new at Peenemunde on the pilot-controlled V-4?" The leader twirled his gold pen, his eyes trying to detect a dent in Zeller's armour.

"The problem lies with the turbojet engine. Dr. von Braun feels that it will take anywhere between three to six months before it will function properly and be ready to fit into the fighter."

"Too long, Herr Doctor."

"My sentiments exactly, Herr Reichsfuehrer."

"What are you going to do about it?"

Zeller cleared his throat. "What can I do, Herr Reichsfuehrer? It is out of my control, and is not my department. The engines are not tested at Peenemunde."

Himmler grunted, easing up on Zeller. "Yes, that is true. Anything else that might be of interest to me?"

"Yes. I want out, Herr Reichsfuehrer."

"What was that?"

"I am not a spy. It is far too difficult to work on a top secret Luftwaffe project while next door to the V-2 compound, constantly patrolled by the SS. I thought we were all on the same side."

"So you want out, do you?"

Zeller pursed his lips. "Yes."

Himmler calmly turned in his chair to the safe behind him. He played with the combination, until the safe popped open. Himmler extracted a file and slapped it on the desk. He spread it slowly as if it were a precious religious document. "Zeller, you are so naive. Look it at! Your file, Herr Doctor, regarding your adulterous relationship with the Berlin prostitute who you were so highly fond of. You've managed to hide it from everybody except me, Herr Zeller. Go ahead, deny it. You can't."

"I won't try." Zeller was crushed. He found no point in looking through the paperwork or defending himself. Himmler knew too much. "It was a mistake I made some time ago."

"Yes, it was. Your first year of marriage." Himmler retrieved the file, returning it to the safe. "Your family doesn't have any inkling, do they?" The leader waited for an answer that never came. "I didn't think so. It would be a shame should they find out, now that your wife is reported missing."

"Yes, it would be a shame," Zeller admitted.

"Therefore, you will continue to be my eyes at Peenemunde West, Herr Zeller. Don't worry about the SS guards, because you are the reason I do not have to send them into the Luftwaffe compound. Now, leave me."

Red-faced, Zeller saluted, spun, and headed for the door.

"Zeller?"

The scientist stopped and cocked his head at the SS leader. "Yes, Herr Reichsfuehrer?"

Himmler's voice reached an octave higher, when he said, "What do you know about a group called the Order of the Knights of National Socialism?"

Zeller was caught unprepared, but quickly recovered. "Never heard of them, Herr Reichsfuehrer. Who are they?"

"Never mind. Go."

Berlin

Bormann and Zeller walked in the Chancellery garden. Overhead, rain clouds began to form. The day was chilly. It was quiet in the capital city.

"What exactly is titanium?" Hitler's secretary asked the scientist.

Zeller took a breath, hands behind his back, staring at the ground. "A lightweight, silver-grey metal, Herr Reichsleiter. It is strong, a much higher strength-weight ratio than steel, and noncorrosive in salt water. It is nearly as hard as diamonds, and has a melting point of over 3000 degrees Fahrenheit. Exactly what is needed for the larger version of the Messerschmitt V-4 interceptor and her anticipated supersonic speeds."

"And they just happened to stumble upon this titanium in the Antarctic?"

"Yes, Herr Reichsleiter."

"Does Himmler know?"

"No. At least I didn't tell him. He did, however, question me about the Order."

"He did? What did he say?"

"He asked me whether I had heard of them."

"And you said?"

"I said I didn't."

"Did he believe you?"

"Yes, I think he did."

"Are you certain he does not suspect you have been reporting to me?"

"Yes, I am. He knows I make excursions to Berlin to see the Fuehrer. That is all."

"What do you think of our illustrious leader, Adolf the Great, now?" Bormann smirked.

"He. . . he has changed. . . He is an old man. Very sick."

"That's putting it mildly. He is blaming everybody. His generals, Goering, Himmler. You name them, he blames them."

Everybody but himself, thought Zeller. "I heard it all, Herr Reichsleiter."

"What did he say to you? Can you remember word for word?" Bormann then pulled out a pad of paper and began to jot down Hitler's conversation with the scientist. After some minutes, Bormann said, "So, it is the Fuehrer's opinion that the morale of the German people is still high?"

"Yes, it is, Herr Reichsleiter."

Bormann put the pad away. He would transfer the notes later to his *tagebuch.* "So. . . how much of this titanium have they found?"

"Enough to build perhaps a thousand Messerschmitt V-4's, Herr Reichsleiter. But there is one tiny complication," Zeller winced.

"That is?"

"The difficulty and expense of separating this vein of titanium from the ores in which it is found."

"I see."

"Titanium is still a new metal. It was discovered only 150 years ago, and wasn't first refined until just recently at Luxembourg—1932 or '33, I believe."

Bormann looked up to the darkening sky. "This might be a touchy subject, but how is your wife, Karl? Is she—?" he stopped short.

Zeller noticed that he was called by his first name, the first time Bormann had ever done so. What was Bormann up to? "She is. . . missing," he lied. Only he, his wife, and von Braun would know the truth. "I have a friend in the government who is keeping me informed of the situation. She is. . . presumed dead."

"I'm sorry. Your parents?"

"They were out of Dresden at the time," Zeller replied, after a long thought. "Visiting in the country."

Bormann seemed to actually care. "Good. Good. At least they were lucky. Dreadful, that's what it was. Give my compliments to them."

"I certainly will, Herr Reichsleiter. Thank you for asking."

Zeller caught early reports from insiders of the Allied bombing of Dresden that had occurred in the week. It was horrifying, to say the least. During a series of massive raids deployed by the British and Americans that had lasted for three days, over 50,000 people died, most of them in a fierce firestorm that raged through the historical city containing some of the greatest architecture in Europe. Dresden was no more. The last Zeller heard, the city was still smouldering.

What was next? Berlin? As if it had not been hard hit already.

Zeller remembered, with a cringe, what a major bombing was like, when parts of Peenemunde were razed by British RAF Lancasters in August, 1943. Eight hundred died. Many of the V-2 facilities were destroyed, forcing the government to move much of the operation to other parts of the country, mainly underground. Then the meddling started. Days after the bombing, Himmler had wrestled all production and deployment of the V-2 rocket out of the hands of von Braun's immediate superior, Walter Dornberger. The following spring, von Braun was arrested by the Gestapo and imprisoned at Stettin for declaring that his main interest in developing the V-2 was for space travel rather than a Nazi military weapon for winning the war. Only Munitions and Armaments Minister Albert Speer had enough influence to release him. Oh, how Zeller hated Himmler. How could he lock up the greatest scientific mind of the century?

Rain began to fall. They walked each other nearer to the Fuehrerbunker's entrance. Bormann stopped the scientist well back of the sentry. "For security reasons, it's best we do not pledge our support of the Order as brothers in the great cause." Bormann studied Zeller from head to foot in one quick glance. "Keep a stiff upper lip, as the British say."

Zeller was unmoved by Bormann's humour. "What is there to look forward to, Herr Reichsleiter?"

"Plenty," Bormann smiled. "Plenty. Will you dine with us this evening at the Fuehrerbunker?"

"Us, Herr Reichsleiter?"

"Yes. My dear friend, Manja, will be joining me soon."

You devil, thought Zeller. Cheating on your wife, again. Some things never change. "Sorry, Herr Reichsleiter. I cannot. I am due back at Peenemunde. There is much to do."

"I'm sure there is."

Then the rain began to fall with a vengeance.

The two men threw themselves to the snow upon hearing the first sound of the aircraft over the rocky cliff. On their stomachs, their white suits blending with the snow, they observed the four-engine monster climbing into the mist covering the northern peninsula.

"Do you think they saw us, old chap?"

"Not a chance." He pulled a pair of binoculars from his bulky backpack and held them to his eyes, adjusting the focusing ring with his thick mittens. He watched the aircraft bank and turn away from them, a good half-mile in the distance. Then he caught the markings. No armament. Polar camouflage of white-blue sky. Churchill called it, "the scourge of the Atlantic." The Focke-Wulf FW 200c Condor had a range of almost 3,000 miles and had disposed of or crippled tons of Allied ships in the Battle of the Atlantic.

"German?"

"Bloody damn right, old boy," the man with the binoculars replied. "She's a Condor. Jerry is around here somewhere, just as we suspected. We had better inform London."

The other man nodded, delighted that their three-day expedition was successful. Back to base at the far end of the peninsula.

The young couple found their way to MI-6 headquarters the next morning and arrived at 9 o'clock sharp. In a smoky conference room on the second floor, they met two men, Wesley's horseface boss, Jack Dorwin of the OSS, and Roberta's superior, Colonel Raymond Lampert of MI-6, section head of Enigma Operations, involved in the breaking of the German ciphers since 1941.

Wesley Hollinger extended his hand to Lampert. "Colonel, it's been some time. Good to see you again."

The couple pulled up chairs around a polished, circular table, Roberta neatly tucking her dress under her legs.

Lampert nodded, a smoking pipe in his mouth. "Good morning, Wesley. How have you been, lad?"

"Hanging in there. You? I thought you were going to retire last month."

"Too busy."

Dorwin lit a new cigar and began the briefing. "I want to read to the both of you an Associated Press article found in the *New York Tribune*, January 2, 1945. *'Now it seems, the Nazis have thrown something new into the night skies over Germany. It is the weird, mysterious 'Foo Fighter' balls, which race alongside the wing of Beaufighters flying intruder missions over Germany. Pilots have been encountering this eerie weapon for more than a month in their night flights. No one apparently knows what this sky weapon is. The balls of fire appear suddenly and accompany the planes for miles. They seem to be radio-controlled from the ground, so intelligence reports reveal.'* Etcetera, etcetera. You can read the rest for yourselves. Here."

Hollinger took the newspaper from his superior. "Thank you."

"This Nazi secret weapon has come to Allied attention," Dorwin continued. "It is serious enough to open a joint Anglo-American file on it. Effective immediately, your job—the both of you—will be to monitor all information pertaining to this. . . weapon. And keep it classified."

"The two of us? Together?"

Dorwin nodded. "Yes, Wesley."

"A combined Allied operation," Hollinger said.

"A little overly dramatic. But, yes."

"Why us?"

"MI-6 and the OSS want someone the two organizations feel is qualified and can trust to work together. Compare notes, that sort of thing."

"Just as you two have done in the past," Lampert added.

"But can we trust each other?" Roberta grinned.

Hollinger turned to his wife. "It's come to this, has it? The secret is out. Now they know why I married you. To get ahead in the Intelligence world."

"Oh, do shut up," she replied.

"Yes, ma'am."

"Of course," Dorwin said, "we will take into consideration Roberta's delicate condition."

"I beg your pardon. I wouldn't show any favouritism just because she's great with child," Hollinger laughed.

"You're asking for it," Roberta snapped.

Dorwin turned to Lampert. "Were they always like this when they were in MI-6?"

"Worse," Lampert replied. "But we got used to it."

65

"What kind of weapon are we referring to, sir?" Roberta asked Lampert. "What do we know about it?"

"A new high-speed fighter, faster than anything before."

Hollinger suddenly remembered the president's words on the same subject. "Is it a jet or another rocket fighter like the Me-163 Komet. . . or what?"

"We don't know. It might even be a new ground-to-air missile. It's your job to find out. Some airmen have already seen it in combat. We will provide you with names. It would be wise to interview them. Roberta the RAF. You, Wesley, the Army Air Forces."

Hollinger handed back the newspaper. "Foo Fighters, huh? How'd they get a kooky name like that?"

Dorwin spoke up. "As near as we can figure, it's derived from a Smoky Stover comic strip. Someone in it had said something like, *where there's foo, there's fire.*"

"Cute," Hollinger said.

"When do you want us to start on this new assignment?" Roberta asked.

Lampert and Dorwin glanced at each other.

"Immediately," Dorwin answered.

Hollinger said, "Of course this means we need a codename."

The others agreed.

An idea suddenly mounted in Wesley Hollinger's mind. "How about. . . the Foo File?"

"Brilliant, Wesley," Lampert smiled. "I do like that. Yes, I do."

"What a mind. That's why I married him," Roberta said, shaking her head. "How do you come up with these things on such short notice?"

"Just comes natural," Hollinger frowned with a hint of a smile.

Eight

Himmler felt betwixt and between when he received his instructions from Hitler in Berlin to move the entire Peenemunde complex underground to the Werra region in the Thuringia Mountains, near the remote-controlled V-4 assembly line.

Mittlewerk was the prime suggested location. Himmler thought about it for a moment, dropping the telephone receiver into its cradle. Fine. It made sense. The Russian Red Army was less than one hundred miles to the east of Peenemunde. The top secret projects had to be kept away from the Russians. What would that pig Goering think of this latest development? His pet—the pilot-controlled V-4—would have to go too. Where? To the same sector? If so, the projects would be too far from Himmler's command post. That part he didn't like.

The second option—a Hitler suggestion—was worse. *Destroy the evidence.* Himmler wouldn't even consider it. They couldn't do that! Time was running out. He thought of *the Order.* To hell with the Order, whoever they were, and whatever their purpose. If it was earlier in the war, he'd follow it up. Not now. No time. One of his agents had heard the name in passing in a Berlin tavern, anyway. Oftentimes what one hears in a tavern over a few drinks doesn't mean anything. Himmler had more important things on his mind. It was up to him to make things happen for himself. He had no choice now. His own skin was at stake. He had put it off too long. Surely Eisenhower or Montgomery would listen? Only Nazi secret weapons would do it. They were the collateral.

Himmler pressed the button on his intercom.

"Yes, Herr Reichsfuehrer," his adjutant answered from the next room.

"Two things. First, I want a line open to Doctor von Braun at Peenemunde. Immediately."

"Yes, Herr Reichsfuehrer. The other?"

"Contact Count Bernadotte of the Swedish Red Cross in Stockholm by cable."

"With what instructions, Herr Reichsfuehrer?"

"Tell him that I wish to speak to him—in person—at his earliest convenience."

"As you wish, Herr Reichsfuehrer."

PEENEMUNDE

When Karl Zeller burst into Wernher von Braun's office in Haus 4 of the V-2 compound at noon, von Braun already had the news.

"I just got off the phone with Goering," von Braun explained. "He will be arriving in two days. So will samples of this titanium discovery. There will be an all-out effort to construct the new V-4 prototype."

"Heaven help us."

"That's not all. They're moving the V-4 testing from Peenemunde West." Von Braun walked to the window and swept the grounds through tired eyes. The sixty to eighty-hour work weeks were taking their toll on the human manual on future space travel.

"Where to?"

"The same general area as the V-2 equipment. If it goes."

"What do you mean, if?" Zeller joined his friend by the window.

"Politics. Need I say more?"

"Will it still be under Luftwaffe control?"

"Yes. Goering wants it to go after the V-2's. That. . . might not be possible, with how things are moving along. What did Himmler say to this transfer of the V-2's?"

"Not very much, to me," Zeller replied.

"Me neither. Except—"

"*You*? I'm confused."

"Relax. I've spoken with both Himmler and Goering this morning. Himmler must know then. He's caught in the middle, like I am."

"Wernher, please, tell me what's happening?"

"I'm faced with a predicament, Karl."

"What kind of predicament?"

"I have received two different sets of orders from two different high-ranking people in the SS. Himmler's appointee, V-2 Director General Hans Hammler has ordered me to move everything relating to the missiles south."

"That's correct. That's the news I have. So?"

"The SS Gauleiter for Pomerania, which includes Peenemunde, ordered me not twenty minutes ago to blow everything up so it wouldn't fall into Russian hands. He is probably on the phone to Berlin as we speak, trying to convince the Fuehrer to such a course of action."

Zeller was shocked. "That's absurd! All this technology, all these years of work up in smoke!"

Von Braun raised a finger. "I don't intend to see that happen. The V-2 and the V-4 will be spared the trash heap."

"I know you. You have a plan. What are you going to do?"

"For two weeks, Dieter and Bernhard have made mimeographed copies of all V-2 and V-4 documents."

"They have?"

"Yes. They intend to hide them in an abandoned mine in the Harz Mountains, and blast the entrance shut."

Zeller flashed a smile. Dieter Huzel and Bernhard Tessman were two of von Braun's trusted aides. Good men. The best. "Excellent plan. But what then?"

"Then, Karl, we would seek out our old friends, the Americans."

"Ah. I like that part the best."

"I thought so. The Americans, I'm sure, will help us once more. And why not. ITT shipped us parts for our V-2's. The American military wants what we have. Look over there. See those trucks arriving at the gate?"

Zeller drew a breath and saw a long line of one-ton trucks roaring across the grounds. "What is this?"

"I've taken it upon myself to begin the move myself."

"By whose authority?"

"Heinrich Himmler, of course."

Zeller folded his arms, his eyes on the driver of one truck approaching one of the buildings. "So, for some strange reason, Himmler wishes to see *Projekt Equinox* and the V-2's continue."

Von Braun agreed. "That is for certain, my friend. Uncle Heine is up to something."

"Wernher?"

"Yes, Karl?"

"I know I'm sounding like an echo, but will you please reconsider and join the Order? It would be for your benefit."

"Never. I told you that before! Politics does not interest me in the least."

EAST ANGLIA, ENGLAND—FEBRUARY 19

Art Tooney seemed embarrassed at first to be interrogated in the small room on his bomber base by this well-dressed American with the custom suit and silk tie who was of age to be in the service and wasn't. This, especially after the gunner had just returned from a horrendous bomber mission to the Ruhr Valley, where he saw four planes in his group shot out of the sky. He was exhausted, dehydrated, and a little annoyed. And he wanted to sleep for a day.

The man asked, "Sergeant Art Tooney?"

"Yeah. Who might you be?"

The handsome man had pocket identification and slapped it on the table. "Wesley Hollinger is my name. OSS."

"Really?" The airman sat up, rubbing his eyes and forehead. He was unimpressed. "American Intelligence? That right?"

"Right."

"Swell. Is this about that new fighter the Jerries have?"

Hollinger grinned, as he pulled a file from his briefcase. This would be the first of his Foo File interviews. "As a matter of fact, it is. Let's start from the beginning," he said, reading from the top sheet. "I'll be quick. I know you want to hit the sack. You're a. . . B-17 ball gunner with 445th Bomb Group. That right?"

"Yeah, that's right. The 99th squadron." Tooney looked around the room, running his hand through his matted hair. "You're not going to laugh at me, are you? There's enough people laughing at me already."

"I promise I won't laugh. I'll hear you out. That's why I'm here. To get the true story. Can I get you a coffee?"

"No thanks. I had a damn good stiff shot of whiskey at debriefing."

Hollinger knew that the liquor was used to loosen the tongues of the bomber crews after trying conditions for the sake of obtaining information for future Eighth Air Force missions. Hopefully, Tooney would still be talking. "Tell me about this," he paused, "Foo Fighter. When did you first see it?"

"So, you know the name?"

"Yes, I do."

"All right." The sergeant gave it heavy thought. "It was January the seventeenth. On a mission to Magdeburg. Our group had crossed the German coast. Jerry FW-190's came up to greet us. Then shortly after that, I saw something going in and out of the clouds."

"A Foo Fighter?"

"Yeah, I guess."

"How far away was it?"

Tooney appeared to judge the distance in his mind by shutting his eyes briefly. "Two hundred yards, I guess."

Hollinger began to take notes on a pad. "Describe it."

"Small."

Hollinger pondered the Me-163 Komet for a moment. It was not a big fighter. "How small, exactly?"

"Well. . . not as big as a regular German fighter. Half the size, I'd say. Son of a bitch, was she moving."

"How fast would you estimate?"

"Too hard to tell. Faster than the other fighters."

"How fast?"

"I'd say. . . maybe. . . twice as fast, flat out."

Hollinger put down his pencil. "Twice as fast!"

"Yeah, that's what I said. Maybe more. I can tell you this, mister. It flew by so damn quick that I'm still wondering if it even happened or what."

"Anybody else in your crew see it?"

"Yeah, the tail gunner. All he saw was a chunk of metal whiz by. So he said."

Hollinger looked strangely at the nervous young boy with the pasty hair, freckles, and air force hat clutched in his hands. Twice as fast as the other fighters meant somewhere over six hundred miles per hour. Hell, he's talking about an aircraft faster than the speed of sound. "What else can you tell me about it?"

"It didn't have any wings. It was round."

Wesley stared at the ball gunner. "Round!"

"Yeah, round. And that's a fact."

Hollinger leaned back in his chair. "*Round.*"

"You're just like the rest of them. You don't believe me."

Wesley recovered, and said, "Don't get me wrong. I'm not insinuating that. You mean round. . . say. . . like a ball."

"No."

"No? What then? I don't get your drift."

Tooney played with his hands to describe the object. "Round like a plate. . . or the lid of a tin can. It was like the top of a tin can with a stump on it. Kind of like a spinning top."

"The stump was a cockpit, I take it."

"It didn't look like no cockpit to me, Mr. Hollinger. It didn't have any glass. At least, I didn't think it had glass."

Hollinger immediately suspected a radio-controlled machine. "That's interesting. No glass in the cockpit," he observed, writing on the pad. "How close did it fly past your bomber?"

"Oh," the gunner said, "fifty feet. Right under us."

"Did you catch any markings on it?"

"Are you kidding? At that speed!"

Hollinger sensed the airman's annoyance. "That's it?"

"Yes, siree. Excuse me, but I have to hit the hay before I drop. It's been a long day."

"Of course. Thanks. Thanks loads," Wesley said, shaking hands with Tooney.

The ball gunner threw his cap on his head and shrank away, leaving Wesley Hollinger to his own crazy thoughts. "Round!" he muttered to himself before he packed up his briefcase and left the room. He remembered the intercepted radio dispatches he had read a few weeks before that indicated new call signs and codenames out of Loebitz airfield. And there was no communications with the pilots. Could they really be the radio-controlled machines?

"Round," he repeated in the hall. *Whoever heard of a round aircraft?*

BIRKENHAIN

Heinrich Himmler, wearing horn-rimmed glasses and a field-grey uniform void of decorations, received Count Folke Bernadotte of the Swedish Red Cross, nephew to King Gustav, at his SS Headquarters.

"I want to know," Himmler began, "if you will be a mouthpiece for peace on the German behalf with the Western Allies, should the moment present itself?"

The middle-aged official paused and answered. "I will do what I can, although I cannot speak for the Allies. I would, however, want something in return from you."

"Name it."

"You must release all Scandinavian prisoners in your concentration camps, should a deal be struck."

Himmler hesitated. "It's possible."

Bernadotte folded his legs in the chair across from Himmler, then asked, "Do you not think it pointless to continue this war with Hitler at the helm? Why do you not seize power yourself, now?"

Himmler shook his head. "No. I could not do that. I took an oath to the Fuehrer. As a soldier and a German, how can I betray him? I have built the SS and the Gestapo on loyalty. I would be abandoning that basic principle."

"I've heard differently about your loyalty to the Fuehrer." When Himmler didn't answer, Bernadotte readied himself to leave.

"Just a moment," Himmler said.

"Yes, Herr Reichsfuehrer."

"If I should release your Scandinavian prisoners, I should want some compensation."

"Such as?"

"I insist that the Danish and Norwegian underground refrain from further sabotage."

"I can't promise you that."

"Then there's nothing I can do."

Bernadotte chuckled. "Herr Reichsfuehrer, you do not have too many choices. You are in a frightening position. You are losing the war and won't last out the year. You will have to bend first. Not me."

Nine

The airfield loomed silent. Reichmarshall Hermann Goering and Wernher von Braun paced along the runway of the Luftwaffe test site, discussing the V-4 situation, the two matching each other stride for stride. A raw, icy breeze blew off the Baltic, chilling them to the bone, despite the bright mid-morning sun.

The titanium had arrived by Condor aircraft that week. Goering wanted to see the new pilot-controlled secret prototype once the metal was refined and put to good use on it. Von Braun seemed to think that the new fighter was only weeks away from completion. A full team was toiling on the V-4, twenty-four hours a day. They spoke of the different phases of development—fire control system, armament testing, performance and handling, intensive flight test program. Each aspect would all have to be stepped up in record time. Good news, the doctor reported, the turbojet engine problems with the compressor had been overcome by the technicians near Berlin. The airflow was running smooth.

Goering looked pleased.

They both stopped to see the last of the V-2 compound next door being shipped off by the fleet of trucks. By evening, the site would be completely vacated. Only a few hundred people were still employed at Peenemunde, most of them at the Luftwaffe project. In the last few days hundreds of trucks had loaded V-2 rocket parts, equipment, and documents and migrated south.

"Has the new V-2 site been determined?" Goering asked.

"Yes," von Braun replied. "Bleicherode, in the Harz Mountains."

"Slight change of plans, then? Not Werra?"

"No."

"The V-4 project will remain until the prototype is finished. Then ship everything out to a location I am in the midst of securing, near the assembly line for the smaller models."

Von Braun nodded, his hair waving in the breeze. He was shocked by Goering's worsening physical condition since their last meeting in December, his voice and body shaking more with each passing month. "And Himmler, what does he have to say to this latest piece of information?"

Goering shrugged. "What can he say? The Luftwaffe is in charge. Not him. I know he's itching to know what we're up to. We can always spread a rumour. We could say we're testing a larger radio-controlled model. Or, better yet, a V-1 launched from a bomber. Anything to keep him out of our hair."

Von Braun shook his head, thinking of Zeller and his association with the SS leader. "It's no use. I'm sure Himmler must know by now. How could he not? His guards have surrounded the place for months. What I can't figure out, Herr Reichmarshall, is why has Himmler been left out of all this? He knows all aspects of the V-2 operation, but the pilot-controlled V-4 prototype we have to keep to ourselves."

"Because I want it that way, Herr Doctor! The Reichsfuehrer thinks he has to stick his nose everywhere. I was the one who kept him out, on Hitler's orders."

Von Braun backed off, squinting in the sunshine. What did it matter? Himmler knew, anyway. "Yes, Herr Reichmarshall."

"Our new Alpine compound will once again be patrolled by Luftwaffe guards on the inside, SS guards on the outside. I spoke to the Fuehrer on the matter, and he assured me that *Project Equinox* will remain under my control."

"Herr Reichmarshall, how close are the Russians?" von Braun asked, bluntly.

Goering wished he could avoid the question. He looked away nervously to the Baltic sand dunes on the horizon, the direction the Red Army would be coming. He brought his hands together to make one giant, white-knuckled fist. "Seventy miles."

"In that case, we had better move swiftly on the prototype."

"Yes. And I must return to Karinhall."

"I will see you to your limousine, Herr Reichmarshall."

LONDON

That evening three men and an attractive redhead woman convened in a smoky conference room on the second floor at MI-6 Headquarters.

"Seven interviews each, I understand," Jack Dorwin said, puffing furiously on his cigar.

"That's correct, sir," Wesley Hollinger replied.

Roberta nodded. "Exactly."

"Let's hear it. What do you have?" Colonel Lampert wanted to know. "Did you compare notes as we had asked?"

"We did," Roberta said. "After you," she gestured to her husband.

Hollinger cleared his throat and began. "Here's the gist of it. We have compiled consistent stories—a pattern—to what the airmen saw. In every case, the men were reluctant to tell their stories to us."

"Why?" Dorwin asked.

"Simply because they thought they'd be laughed at."

"I see. Continue. Please."

"OK. First, the speed of this fighter. . . is. . . get this. . . somewhere well over one thousand miles per hour."

"Astonishing!" Lampert uttered, removing the pipe from his mouth.

"Impossible," Dorwin said. "No fighter can go that fast."

"We have the information, sir. The V-2's can do two thousand easily, and then some. Why *can't* the Germans find a fighter that matches such speeds?"

"You're talking about a fighter, not a missile."

Roberta tugged her husband's sleeve. They had both sensed beforehand that they would get this sort of reaction.

Roberta took a deep breath and said, "Mr. Dorwin, you and the colonel asked Wesley and me to interview the airmen, compare notes and evaluate this new Nazi fighter—whatever it is. And now we're telling you. In most cases, the airmen saw this *thing* scream by so fast they thought it was a bullet. The shape in half the case studies is similar. Round, and thin. Like a plate or saucer. Half the size of normal fighters. No cockpit, merely a piece of metal in the middle. On top. In five of the situations, the fighter let loose a spray of some sort. No bullets. No cannon. In two of those cases, the spray went straight for an engine exhaust of two B-17 bombers in the same flight. Both times the bombers exploded in mid-air. Four of my seven personal interviews were night-time sightings. Every time the eyewitnesses reported that this machine glowed orange all around its circumference. And, from all the information at our disposal, we believe these machines are not pilot-operated, but quite possibly radio-controlled, as the *New York Tribune* article reported."

"From where?" Lampert queried. "Other planes in the air?"

"Like the newspaper article stated, from the ground. Thanks to some sophisticated radar system that can bring the fighters to point-blank range."

Dorwin and Lampert stared at each other, calmly, eyes large, not saying a word.

"This, gentlemen," Hollinger added, his voice steady, "is another one of those things that we had better get our hands on before the damn Russians do, along with the V-1, and the V-2. If we don't, the Russians will be miles and years ahead of us, and—"

Lampert stood. "You've made your point, I trust, young man," he said, "and we thank you, Wesley and Roberta. Leave us with the. . . Foo File. You're both off the case."

Hollinger grunted. "Really?"

"Yes."

"And. . . that's it?" Hollinger said. He couldn't understand it. A week of solid work, the interviews, thousands of words on paper. They had only started. And all over with so quickly, as if it had never happened in the first place. "If you say so. Let's go," he said to his wife.

PEENEMUNDE WEST

Zeller placed the last of the large blueprint papers in the printing frame, under the last of the original drawings. He flicked on the strong light for the required time, then flicked it off. He removed the blueprint paper and slid it into the tray of water. Before his eyes, he saw the paper turn blue in the spots where the light had activated the chemicals on the sheet, and white where it had not. Waiting several minutes, he allowed the sheet to dry. Then he gave it another shot of light.

It had been a long process. Zeller now had exact copies of the new, pilot-controlled V-4 drawings.

Bormann lit a cigarette in the Chancellery garden.

"I thought you quit," Goering asked him, twirling his baton.

"I did. But I started again. Nerves, you know."

Goering knew all about nerves. "This has been hard on all of us."

"Yes, it has. Let's walk some more."

They came to a stop in the centre of the garden.

"How is the Fuehrer?" asked the Luftwaffe leader.

"You'll see for yourself when he finally wakes. The drug is working better than expected. It seems to mix well with his chocolates. A lethal combination." Bormann laughed. "Have you come to a decision?"

"Yes."

"Well, must you keep me in suspense?"

Goering's eyes were bright with vigour. "Count me in, Bormann."

Bormann exhaled a cloud of smoke. "You won't regret it. I will make contact with the Americans."

"Are you sure this will work?"

"Positive, Herr Reichmarshall. They will listen to proposals put forward by men of our calibre. As long as we hold *Projekt Equinox* and the V-4 in reserve. And don't forget what we have on Dulles and the greedy American companies assisting us since the war began. The list is endless."

"Do you have proof of the transactions?"

"Yes, of course I have proof. Months ago, I locked some shipping documents away in a Swiss vault. Bills of lading and invoices that follow a path from the United States to Argentina to Spain to Switzerland."

"How on earth did you get these documents?"

"Swiss and American friends loyal to the cause."

"You mean loyal to their own bank accounts."

"Yes, that's probably more like it. Furthermore, you yourself, Herr Reichmarshall, have a cousin in America, Hugo von Rosen, who is a partner in a Philadelphia company under Swedish control that has supplied us with ball bearings via South America for five years. I have in my possession some of those documents too."

"How do you know about Hugo?"

"My Swedish connections, again."

"A lot of good that will do me now, having a cousin overseas," Goering said. "So, you will hand the Americans the other military plans first? The V-1s, the V-2s, the jets?"

"Yes, just as I told you before. But our biggest problem could be Himmler. We must keep him at arm's length."

"I will," Goering assured his brother in the Order. "I have the Fuehrer's ear in that matter. Himmler and his SS will not be running the new V-4 project. The SS are not allowed inside the compound."

Bormann nodded, then asked, "Did you close up your estate?"

"No, not yet."

"Where will you go when you do?"

"Berchtesgaden. My family is already there."

"That's good thinking, Goering. Close to Switzerland. Easier for an escape over the border."

"Yes. And closer to the advancing Americans, should anything go wrong with the OSS talks."

"And why should anything go wrong?"

"Only a precaution on my part," Goering said. "Nothing is for certain these days."

"Very true."

"According to Wehrmacht reports, General Patton's Third Army is heading that way. He will reach there before the Russians or the British."

You hope, thought Bormann. "Good plan."

"What will you do?"

"Stay with the Fuehrer, of course," Bormann replied.

Goering put his hands on his hips. "Have you lost your mind?"

"No."

"But why stay?"

"I can't leave him. It will look far too suspicious for me to up and leave now."

"But don't you know the Fuehrer will not surrender. He will hold out till the end. By then it may be too late for you to escape. The Russians are sure to reach Berlin before the British or the Americans. They will surround the city."

"I'll have to take my chances." Bormann glanced at his watch. "You had better go below. The Fuehrer will rise soon. Blood brother, Goering."

Goering stood erect, baton by his side. "Blood brother, Bormann," he said, well overdone in enthusiasm.

It seemed ridiculous to Bormann, as he watched Goering proceed to the Fuehrerbunker entrance. The secretary still didn't trust Goering, and the feeling, Bormann was certain, was mutual. So who was kidding who?

He stomped the cigarette into the soft earth.

So, he's waiting for Patton, is he? Bastard!

Ten

He was a dream come true to the Allied press. They called him "Old Blood and Guts." He wore a pair of ivory-handled .45-calibre Frontier Model revolvers on his hips. He used profanity during the day, then never forgot to read his Bible at night. Everywhere he ventured, he took his bull terrier, Willie, with him. He was a man of action. He was also a terror to the Nazis. With lightning sweeps, his Sherman tanks had chased the enemy across the hot, dry North African desert and through the soft underbelly of Sicily, always in a race to beat the British general he so loathed, Bernard Montgomery.

To his friends he was George or Georgie. People either loved him or hated him. He talked too much, often telling everyone within earshot that the Allied High Command was denying him the full glory of early Allied victory. Along the way, he had slapped out two of his own soldiers, thus angering scores of his superiors, including his friend, Supreme Commander of the Allied Forces, General Dwight Eisenhower. He was an embarrassment to Eisenhower and Montgomery, who both tried to bring Georgie under control by under-supplying him so that Montgomery could advance at a quicker pace through France to give the British press something to write about.

Fifty-nine-year-old General George S. Patton Jr. was the commanding officer of the mighty American Third Army, which had captured so many German prisoners in France that the authorities didn't know what do with them all. Since his army had been deployed in the French campaign in August 1944, Patton lived by one motto: "On to the Rhine."

And, of course, he had to make a game of it and beat the British—that cocky, egotistical Montgomery—there too, as he had done so triumphantly at Messina in Sicily.

Midday, at his command post, the six-foot-plus Patton was in a celebrating mood. His Third Army had taken Trier on the Moselle in violation of Eisenhower's original orders. Outside, distant artillery popped.

"General, sir. These have just come through."

Patton received two dispatches from his adjutant. The general sat down next to another chair taken by Willie and opened the first sealed envelope. It was from one of his personal spies, a newspaper correspondent he knew who had been following the Third Army advance through France. The reports of the German prisoners were true, the writer felt. Grumbling, Patton folded the dispatch and placed it in a side trouser pocket of his immaculate uniform. He rubbed his thin, silvery hair. He knew the Americans had several prisoner camps in liberated France, many taken over by the French army. Held mostly outdoors in barbed-wire enclosures with little or no food or water, thousands of German soldiers were apparently used for labour, starved and mistreated so terribly that some were dying. Patton had even heard a rumour that relief organizations like the International Red Cross were denied access to the prisoners. A lot of these prisoners were captured by his Third Army, and now they were facing horrible, unsanitary conditions. Although he had beaten them on the battlefield, he felt responsible for the German soldiers. There were German prisoners in Ike's hands who were starving to death, and the Supreme Commander, so it seemed, was doing nothing about it.

Patton shook his head in disgust. He was peeved. Blasted, they were fighting the wrong enemy. The Russians were next. The Western Allies had to take Europe before the Russians did. But Ike couldn't see it. Too bad Ike was more a politician than he was a soldier. This war was grooming him for the presidency.

Patton opened the second dispatch, read it, and chuckled. What a joke! For the second time in two days, Eisenhower was ordering Patton to bypass Trier because it would supposedly take at least four divisions to do the job.

The general stood and faced his adjutant squarely. "Send this message off to General Eisenhower's headquarters," he said in his high-pitched voice. "Right away."

"Yes, sir."

The adjutant grabbed a pencil.

"Tell General Eisenhower that I have taken Trier with two divisions. Stop. What do you want me to do? Stop. Give it back? Stop."

The adjutant grinned, and Patton laughed out loud. "Send it."

"Yes, sir!"

ANTARCTIC

The two-man British search team reached the snowy crest of the ridge, taking the last few feet on their stomachs. Their breath steamed in the frosty air. At first, they couldn't fathom what they saw through their binoculars.

"Will you look at that," one of them said, astonished, glancing at the man-made buildings hundreds of feet nearly straight down. "No wonder our radio controllers couldn't monitor any German communication, tucked away here in this valley."

"Righto, ol' boy. Wonder how long they've been here? From the look of things, probably quite a while, I'd say. Imagine, right under our noses. And we've been on the other side of the peninsula almost two years. Telephone poles, electricity. A whole power station. Blimey, it's a small town. They have the nerve to fly their bloody swastika this far from home."

"Yeah. Guess they didn't expect anybody else to be around."

"Guess not. What's that up the hill?"

"Looks like drilling equipment, ol' boy."

"What would they be drilling out here?"

"Oil, maybe. Minerals."

"They must know something we don't."

"Right you are."

They studied the camp for several moments, edging closer in their white snowsuits to the cliff's edge.

"What do you know, a ploughed runway out there."

"Yeah. Has to be at least a mile long."

"Perfect length for the Condor we saw a little while ago."

"Right. By the way, when do we move in and pay our guests a little visit?"

"As soon as we get the clearance. But we need reinforcements. No telling how many blokes are in there."

"Let's go. Stay down."

"You bet."

LONDON

Roberta Hollinger-Langford was thoroughly confused. "Zurich?" she said.

"Yeah, hereby reassigned. That's what Dorwin told me. Just after lunch." Hollinger threw his suit jacket and fedora on the apartment couch. "Allen Dulles himself, the OSS Director, told him. And those orders came from Donovan."

"How many times have I told you to hang your coat up?"

"Sorry." Hollinger took the coat to the bedroom closet and placed it on a hangar. He threw the hat on the shelf, then returned to his wife's side in the living room. His face was fixed in a frown. "What do you make of it?"

"Don't ask me to think like an American. I only married one."

Hollinger chuckled.

"Maybe it has something to do with the Foo File."

"It's possible." Hollinger shrugged.

"When do you leave?"

"Day after tomorrow."

"For how long?"

Hollinger seemed to be in a fog. "They wouldn't tell me."

Winston Churchill's telephone in his underground war room rang. His Majesty's First Minister lifted the receiver gently, a smouldering cigar in his mouth.

"Sir, it's Colonel Lampert."

"Yes, colonel," Churchill acknowledged.

"Two things, sir. First, our MI-6 search team in Antarctica found what they gather to be a large-scale German mining expedition on the peninsula. They are currently under observation, waiting on our orders."

"What are you waiting for? Send them in, by God! But take them alive. I want those Germans interrogated. Use everything at our disposal, including the truth drugs."

"Yes, sir. Thought you might say that."

"What else?"

"It's Wesley Hollinger."

"What the blazes did he do this time?"

"The OSS is sending him to Switzerland for some unknown reason. Temporary assignment."

Churchill dragged on his cigar, exhaling before he asked, "On whose orders?"

"Donovan's."

"Highly irregular, wouldn't you say, colonel?"

"Yes, isn't it."

"I thought he was working on the Foo File with his wife."

"Not anymore. Dorwin and I decided to cancel it."

"When was this?" Churchill barked. "No one briefed me."

"We did it late yesterday. Nothing new was coming out of it. We'll have to wait and see what our armies uncover once we overrun Germany."

"So, right after the Foo File is canceled, the OSS sends the bloke away."

"Perhaps it's merely a coincidence."

"Or perhaps the Americans will somehow, some way, go back to being Americans, and not Allies."

"What do you mean by that, sir?"

"This, colonel: Maybe they will cut a separate deal with Germany, through those damn money-grabbing Swiss."

"For the technology?"

"Exactly. Bloody Yankees."

"I second that, sir. If what you say turns out to be true."

"Keep me informed, colonel."

"Yes, sir."

Eleven

Area 14 swarmed with activity in the early afternoon once the news broke that the Messerschmitt V-4 Experimental Series 1-2a pilot-controlled, titanium prototype with the new turbojet engine was announced ready for its first outdoors test.

Two men slid the hangar door open. A third man jumped on a truck, started it up, and towed the V-4 fighter onto the tarmac. The scientists stood by the hangar door: von Braun, Zeller, and others in the team that had stayed behind after the V-2 facility had been vacated. Nearly two hundred technicians were milling off to the right near the parking lot.

Von Braun folded his arms over his white smock. He saw the SS guards outside the fenced-in compound eyeing the strange machine. One of them had a set of binoculars to his eyes. "It's no secret anymore," the scientist said. "There's no way of hiding this."

Zeller smiled. "Rest assured," he said. "Someone is on the phone to Himmler as we speak."

They heard footsteps behind them. A pilot in flying gear walked by, nodded at the scientists, crawled over the wing, and got into the fighter through the open hatch. Once in the cockpit, he looked through the small Plexiglas opening to von Braun, sixty feet away.

A loudspeaker blared, "TWENTY. . . NINETEEN. . . EIGHTEEN. . ." The pilot closed the hatch and locked it from the inside.

Zeller leaned towards von Braun. "I can't believe that the technicians constructed this titanium model so quickly."

"See what happens when we're threatened by Berlin?"

"Amazing. Simply amazing. Three weeks. And they sorted out the engine problems too. I just hope we're not bringing it out too soon."

Von Braun frowned at his "Doubting Thomas" cohort. "Both teams worked twenty-four hours a day. Hundreds of people. Besides, it's only a larger version of the radio interceptors. They only had to expand on the blueprints. Now, it's our job to test *this one* and ready it for production."

"FIFTEEN. . . FOURTEEN. . . THIRTEEN. . ."

Zeller handed out the earplugs with five seconds to go.

"FOUR. . . THREE. . . TWO. . . ONE. . ."

On cue from von Braun, the pilot started up the saucer-shaped machine, the latest in the astounding Nazi technical arsenal. With a blast, the twin turbojet caught fire, vibrating the tarmac beneath the scientists' feet. At no time in their lives had anyone here heard a sound this loud and powerful from an aircraft.

They cheered.

The pilot glanced over, grinning.

Von Braun spun his finger around, the signal for the pilot to try the next test procedure. Suddenly, the two turbojet exhausts pointed downwards. The fighter lifted off the tarmac, suspended a few feet in mid-air, turning slightly, slowly, undercarriage down. Then the nose dipped and it moved forward. It remained suspended, wobbling. It lifted higher, then sped smoothly away over the field, banked over the closest runway, and returned to hover over the tarmac.

Von Braun ran a line across his throat. The undercarriage tires touched the tarmac, and the pilot cut the engines. Von Braun was pleased with the speed and the manoeuvrability. The turbojets were certainly healthy. "Next on the agenda, I'll call Reichmarshall Goering and give him the positive report. Karl?"

"Yes, Wernher?"

"Make the arrangements to ship everything out as soon as possible. We are transferring our operation south."

BERLIN

The Fuehrer was in a sombre mood in his underground Fuehrerbunker office. Throwing a chocolate in his mouth, he said to his secretary, "Bormann, I want your advice on an important decision that I will have to face."

Bormann sat up, pen and *tagebuch* in hand. "Me, mein Fuehrer?"

"Yes, you," Hitler replied, his voice raspy, older than his fifty-five years. "I can rely on very few people. It makes me sick. Germany will be left without a leader. Who will be my successor? Hess is mad. *Who*? Himmler? Goebbels? I must decide on whom I shall hand total power over to in an emergency in the event of my death."

Bormann was startled that Hitler was finally admitting the end was near. "I don't. . ." He paused.

"Well?" Hitler asked calmly.

Bormann knew that a civilian choice like himself, Himmler, or Goebbels would not hold water. Those in uniform would not go for it. "I have two in mind, perhaps."

"Let's have them. Quickly."

"Admiral Doenitz is loyal, and has the leadership qualities to represent the Fatherland. He is a military man, widely respected in the Navy."

Hitler gave the suggestion serious thought. "Doenitz is a possibility, yes. The other?"

Bormann held his breath. "May I suggest Goering?"

"What!" the Fuehrer exploded, his placid face reddening. He jumped to his feet with energy he hadn't had in months. "That buffoon. Why would you say him? He's not fit. . . not fit to lead a pig to its trough. I told you before we should have hung him along with his cowardly Luftwaffe."

Bormann began writing. "May I remind you, mein Fuehrer, that you did appoint him your successor in 1940."

Hitler eased up. "I did, didn't I? Well, he's not anymore. That will soon change. Doenitz it is. But keep that to yourself. I will wait until the appropriate time."

"Yes, mein Fuehrer."

"How are the secret weapons coming along? The new V-4, what of it?"

"It has passed its first run-up, mein Fuehrer, at Peenemunde."

"When will it be put into full production?"

"As soon as the facilities are up and running in the Thuringia Mountains."

Hitler began to soften and reminisce. "Look what it's come to. I had a solution to mankind's problems. A New World Order. But I see a new and different order rising up, controlled by financial supermen of strength, power, and prestige. Everyone worldwide will be subject

91

to this elite of the earth. These sons of gods. These kings. We could have put a stop to it, Bormann. I shudder to see the world to come in the next few years."

"Me too, mein Fuehrer," Bormann admitted.

"I know I don't intend to be around for it."

But I, for one, plan to, thought Bormann, writing in his tagebuch, while taking on the expression of the cat that had swallowed the canary. "It's a terrible shame, mein Fuehrer."

Twelve

The OSS director stood, bent over his desk, and reached out his hand to his first visitor of the early afternoon series of appointments. "Good afternoon, Mr. Hollinger. Welcome to Switzerland."

"Thank you, sir."

"Pull up a chair, young man."

"Thank you." Hollinger sat and looked around the large, panelled office, impressed with the spaciousness. It was twice the size of his London office. To the right was a two-foot-square wall clock with long, pewter hands.

"How was your trip?"

Hollinger would never forget the flight. It was the closest he had come to throwing up in the air. "Kind of. . . on the bumpy side."

"How was the weather in Lisbon?"

"Rainy."

"And London."

"Foggy, as always, sir, in March. Director Dorwin sends his regards."

Hollinger smiled at Allen Welsh Dulles, Washington's spymaster in Switzerland, appointed by Roosevelt in 1942. Dulles had a distinct grandfather image. In his fifties, he was tall, statuesque, grey-haired, and wore glasses and a navy, pin-striped suit. A lawyer by trade, he was a product of America's elite, educated at Princeton and George Washington University. Only a few people in the right places knew that in the years leading up to war that he had been a staunch Adolf Hitler supporter.

Dulles sagged into his padded chair, and tapped his ballpoint pen on his desktop. "Mr. Hollinger, do you have any idea why you've been sent here?"

"Not in the least, sir. I'm dying to find out."

"The orders come directly from General Donovan. I don't exactly agree with how this is being done. However, like any good soldier, no matter what the field, I only obey. Furthermore, my name is not to be mentioned in this little undertaking. Do you understand?"

"Yes, sir. I was informed of that already."

"Good. Don't forget it."

Hollinger was suddenly aware of the wall clock ticking. "I will, sir. I mean I won't, sir. I mean. . . you know."

The intercom box on Dulles's desktop buzzed and he pressed a button. "Yes."

"Mr. McCreedy is here, Mr. Dulles," a woman's voice said.

"Thank you. Send him in."

"Yes, sir."

The office door opened.

Dulles turned. "Good afternoon, Mr. McCreedy. You recall Wesley Hollinger from your days together in Washington and London?"

Hollinger turned and stood up. Yes, he knew McCreedy, and he also remembered how much he couldn't stand the man. "Hello again, Tom," he said, coldly.

"Hello, Wesley, old buddy."

They shook hands.

"Get to it," Dulles informed McCreedy. "Kindly brief Mr. Hollinger on the way. Remember, I don't have anything to do with this little scheme."

"Understood, sir."

Outside, the sun was shining brightly, the temperature in the mid-fifties. They hopped into a nearby tavern, where McCreedy downed two stiff drinks to Hollinger's one. Then they walked a few blocks, and entered a private compartment on the train to Lake Lacerne.

Hollinger had disliked Thomas McCreedy from the moment they first met in 1940, during their early cipher training experience at Washington. McCreedy was always too cheerful, too intelligent, too damn political for his thirty years, and he also drank too much, too often. In addition, McCreedy was too weird. Too smart for his own good. Often-times, he was in his own world. He still wore those goofy round glasses with the thick lenses and his hair was still parted in the middle. Born and raised in Virginia, McCreedy majored in accounting and political science at a South Carolina college. His first job out of school saw him at the giant Rockefeller-owned oil firm of Standard Oil. After two years in the business world, he jumped to clandestine work, another one of those handpicked recruits, compliments of the mysterious Mr. Donovan. Currently, McCreedy was a monetary and special affairs specialist for the OSS in Switzerland.

Together, McCreedy and Hollinger looked out the wide window as the train hissed and steamed in the station.

"How's London, old buddy? Been to Piccadilly lately?" McCreedy's speech was slightly slurred.

Hollinger knew McCreedy was referring to the streetwalkers of London. "Come now, I'm a married man, Tom."

"So I hear."

"Yes, and my wife is great with child."

"Congratulations." McCreedy removed a cigarette from a small pocket case. "When's she due?"

"May."

"Still wearing the flashy ties, I see."

"And you? Still single?"

"Engaged. A Swiss girl." McCreedy lit the cigarette with his lighter.

"That's nice. I wish you both all the happiness in the world. OK, let's cut the bullshit." Hollinger turned directly to McCreedy. "What's up, Tom? Dulles didn't look all that happy with my coming here. What is this all about?"

"Are you in for a dilly of an assignment. Dulles has his moods. OK. No, he doesn't like it one bit because Donovan asked for you, an outsider, from London too, above all the agents stationed here."

"So, them's the breaks. I can't help that."

"No, you can't." McCreedy paused. "OK, ever hear of Martin Bormann?"

Hollinger shrugged. "Sure. One of Hitler's henchmen. Don't know that much about him, though."

"Most people don't. Bormann has always kept it that way. Here's the lowdown. He's Adolf Hitler's personal secretary." McCreedy pulled a file from his briefcase, and used it as a guide. "Here's the background check on him. Born June 17, 1900. Joined an artillery regiment in World War One. Served one year in prison for collaborating in the murder of his elementary teacher. In 1929, he married Gerda Buch, the ceremony witnessed by both Adolf Hitler and Rudolf Hess. The couple had ten kids."

"Ten!"

"Yes, ten. And he probably had some illegitimate brats along the way too, the way he's screwed around. Anyway, Bormann became Rudolf Hess's Chief of Staff in 1933. After Hess literally flew the coop in 1941, Hitler abolished Hess's post as Deputy Fuehrer and appointed Bormann to direct the newly created Nazi Party Chancellery. Since then, Bormann has outmanoeuvred all his rivals. For years he's been the most powerful man in Germany, but very few know it because he stays out of the limelight, and is very seldom photographed, unlike Himmler, Goering, Goebbels, and the others. He makes most of Hitler's decisions for him, handles his affairs, and he's hated by the others in the German High Command for his closeness to the Fuehrer. He is also the Nazi contact to some very important Swiss bank accounts. We—the OSS—have heard through a good source in this country that Bormann is willing to cut a deal with us."

"A deal with the enemy?"

"Right."

"What happened to Unconditional Surrender?"

"Hah!" McCreedy chuckled. "Just something that sounds good for the Allied press. There are several deals in the works, Wesley. They all come under the umbrella of what a few of us in the OSS call *Operation Paperclip*. It is our job to get certain Nazis out of Germany before it falls in exchange for their advanced scientific knowledge, such as the V-weapons, the military jet aircraft, and this new aircraft, the Foo Fighter, which you are well aware of from the Foo File."

Hollinger shifted in the seat. He stared earnestly at McCreedy. "I thought that was classified. Only the London office knew of the file's existence."

"Not anymore. Anyway, that's why you're here. You, Wesley, are going to be our American contact in these negotiations with the enemy. And I will assist you."

"The two of us?"

"Yes. Let me emphasize that we here in Switzerland are especially interested in the Foo Fighter."

"I wonder why?"

"Bormann's intermediary is an unnamed member of the Swiss investment firm of Erickson, Fruge, & Company, a family-run bank that handles the accounts for Bormann and other Nazis, not to mention several large American companies. But that's another story. The meetings will take place thirty miles from here in Lake Lucerne. I've been there once. Quite nice, actually. I hope high elevations don't bother you. We'll be up about a mile or more above sea level."

"Don't worry about me, I can take it," Hollinger said.

"There's another wrinkle. A South American country—namely Argentina—has volunteered to take in these Nazis, at a price."

"A piece of the pie? Money? A Swiss account or two?"

"Yes. Therefore, at these meetings will be a representative of Juan Peron, a high-ranking official in Argentina who will probably be the next leader of that country. The man's name is Benito Cocapo."

"So, we get the technology and the scientists, while Argentina gets the dough and hides the leaders."

"Aren't you the perceptive one, Wesley? It'll be an Anglo-Spanish-German consortium of cooperation. An understanding."

"And the press and the public won't suspect a thing."

"Of course not. They never do. Chosen people will take the heat and be punished. Himmler, for example. Bormann's sources have fed us documents to show that Gestapo chief Heinrich Himmler has ordered millions to their deaths in concentration camps. We are promised photos shortly. And we have copies of the written orders from the Fuehrer."

"How do you know Bormann isn't behind these deaths, if he's as close to Hitler as you say he is?" Hollinger asked.

"You always were a straight shooter, Wesley. Good question. I thought of it too. Maybe he is. But that's none of our business right now."

"Just follow orders."

"Right. Wherever they come from."

"Washington, you mean."

McCreedy said, "Or a hell of a lot higher than that."

Hollinger looked at Thomas McCreedy strangely. "You mean the Allies?"

"You are so out of it, Wesley, old buddy. Not unlike every other war, this one is a rich man's war, and a poor man's fight. There are higher powers out there that make the world turn. People who even Roosevelt answers to. Men of money. International Bankers. Wall Street shakers. Oil barons. Steel magnates. These people know no borders and have no morals. Here's one for you. Did you know that Standard Oil, my old employer, has shipped oil to the Nazis all along?"

"They have?"

"Yes, they have. And did you know that Standard Oil, Du Pont, and GM are the only ones who have world rights to tetraethyl lead, a major gasoline additive?"

"I don't get the connection. So? What of it?"

"The Germans were short of it back in 1939."

"I repeat. So?"

"They purchased twenty million dollar's worth of it from Standard Oil, then turned around and attacked Poland to start the war. I saw the paperwork for it. You listen to me. This war was well planned out in the corporate board rooms of New York, London, and yes, even Berlin, all for the sake of power and profit."

"You're nuts. Who the hell in Berlin, of all places, wanted this war to make money?" Hollinger asked.

"Ever hear of I.S. Filberg?"

"Sure have. The German industrial cartel. They were receiving Wall Street loans for their munitions factories before the war."

McCreedy was awestruck. "How did you know that?"

Hollinger remembered the Hess peace initiatives. "Don't ask."

"Geez! I guess I shouldn't. Well, I've got news for you. The loans didn't stop on December 7, 1941. It all comes under *Trading with the Enemy Act*, stamped and approved by Roosevelt himself so that the people who put him in power get rich off this war. All nice and legal. And Dulles is in up to his balls. He loves the Nazis. He always has. He's been the legal advisor for the Anglo-German Schroeder bank."

"Go on. I don't believe it."

"Believe it. Back home in New York, his law partner, De Lano Andrews, is *advising* the Germans as we speak through the New York branch of the Schroeder bank. I know this to be true. I know people on Wall Street. And I'll tell you something else. Dulles was a law partner at Sullivan and Cromwell in the 1920s. They handled all the I.S. Filberg legal paperwork in America. Now do you know why Dulles doesn't want his name mentioned?"

Hollinger didn't like the way the conversation was moving. "Are you telling me that Dulles is a traitor?"

McCreedy shrugged. "Don't let me decide for you. Figure it out for yourself."

The train lurched and began to move.

McCreedy looked across at the slowly disappearing train station platform through the window. "Let's go to the bar. I could use another drink. How's about you?"

"No. I've had enough. Take my advice, you have too. And take my advice on something else."

"Yeah, what?" McCreedy asked.

"Be careful who you talk to about what you know."

Lake Lucerne

The hotel desk clerk handed the sealed white envelope to Hollinger as soon as he and McCreedy checked in. They quickly read the note inside.

Hollinger. See you at the shooting range. Erickson.

"Excuse me?"

"Yes, Mr. Hollinger?" the clerk asked, in German-accented English.

"Is there a shooting range around here?"

"Yes, there is, sir. Proceed to the walkway behind the hotel parking lot. Follow the brick path to the right. It's about a three or four minute walk."

"Thanks."

"Let's settle into our rooms first," McCreedy suggested, puffing on a cigarette.

"Yeah, sure."

Twenty minutes later, they followed the clerk's directions. The brick path opened into a flat, grass clearing where people were trapshooting. The snow on the distant mountains surrounding Lake Lucerne glistened in the sunlight.

Hollinger frowned. "How are we to find him in this?"

"Search me," McCreedy said.

"Do you know what he looks like?"

"Never met him."

"Great." Hollinger took a few deep breaths. They certainly were high up, where the air was indeed thinner.

They strolled down the line of men operating the traps for the shooters. Hollinger was fascinated by the shape of the traps. Round and flat. . . aerodynamically-sound. . . kind of like the Foo Fighters. No wonder they flew out of the machines so fast. Suddenly, one of the marksmen—a blonde woman with long hair tied in the back—fired a shotgun, shattered the clay pigeon flung from the trap, then turned around and strolled over to the agents, shotgun resting on her shoulder.

Hollinger looked her over. She wore slacks, and was in her late twenties, average height, extremely attractive. She had clear, olive skin, wide lips, thin nose, and eyes like two blue crystals. Any man who didn't find her stunning had to be dead.

In English, but hinting of a German accent, she said, "Wesley Hollinger and Thomas McCreedy, I presume." She held out her hand. Her voice was soft, yet business-like. Very professional.

"Yes, we are," Hollinger answered. "I'm Hollinger. This is McCreedy. And who might you be?" he asked.

"Johanna Erickson." Eyes flashing, she shook hands with the two men. There was an upright openness about her as well as a strength to her handshake. "By the look of surprise on your face, you had expected a man. Yes, I shoot traps, and yes, I am the one you will be bargaining with."

"You're Erickson?" Wesley said with a grunt. So, Erickson wasn't a him, but a dame with a very unmasculine shape.

"So, you're *Hollinger.*"

The three chuckled.

"How's our mutual friend, Mr. Dulles?" she asked.

"Fine," replied McCreedy, nudging at his glasses. "Just fine."

"Good shooting out there," Hollinger said, smiling.

"Thank you. You should try it sometime."

"Well," Hollinger said, glancing around at the trapshooting action, "when do we get started on our project?"

"As soon as Cocapo arrives," Erickson informed the Americans. "He'll be coming along within the hour. We will all have dinner together at the hotel, yes?"

"Sure," Hollinger said.

"Now, if you'll excuse me, I want to finish up."

"Don't let us stop you," Wesley muttered.

She smiled with even, white teeth, and displayed a set of dimples. She moved away with an easy, alluring grace that impressed the two Americans.

One good-looker, Hollinger thought, giving her a final once-over.

"Not bad," McCreedy said.

Hollinger shrugged "Ah, so-so."

"You're kidding, right?"

"I'm hitched, remember."

Over wine in a small enclosed booth, away from the others in the room, the meeting of five commenced just after seven that evening.

"Let me get something straight," Hollinger said to the beautiful Johanna Erickson. Her hair was down and parted in the middle, and she now wore a white blouse and dark-green slacks. Hollinger chose to momentarily ignore the short, stubby Benito Cocapo, and his Spanish translator.

"What is that?" she said in an equally-lowered voice.

"Your firm is representing certain. . . Nazi individuals."

"Martin Bormann in this case," she corrected Hollinger from across the table. "He, of course, could not be here in person."

"Obviously."

"Our banking firm will negotiate on his behalf. He insists on us talking directly with the Americans. Not the British or the Russians."

"And Mr. Dulles's name is also our little secret," Hollinger said to Erickson.

"Of course."

"OK, now, where is Bormann?" Hollinger asked.

"In Berlin. By Hitler's side."

"It's only a matter of time before Berlin falls with the Red Army closing in. Will he get out?"

"He expects to."

"He'd better, for our sake and his. When does he plan to do this?"

"I don't know, Mr. Hollinger."

"Too vague. Much too vague." Hollinger shook his head.

She frowned. "What more can I do?"

"He is asking for his freedom in exchange for the recent technical inventions by German scientists. If he doesn't get out, then we will be forced to deal with someone else. But it might be too late by then."

A waiter walked by.

"Quiet," Erickson warned in a muffled voice.

They waited until he was safely on the other side of the room.

"He. . . has. . . contacts. You will have your inventions," she informed Hollinger.

"And you," Hollinger turned to Cocapo, "will take Bormann and whoever in for. . . safekeeping in this three-way transaction, I take it?"

"And we get the rest," McCreedy whispered, lighting a new cigarette.

The two Americans thought of it together. *Operation Paperclip.* Cocapo drank from his wine glass, nodding once as the translator finished speaking in Spanish to him.

"Allow me to clarify things. The OSS are willing to deal on two conditions," Hollinger continued. "One, I see some documents first. Actual blueprints of these inventions."

"That can be arranged, Mr. Hollinger," Erickson said.

"Good. Two, we want the Peenemunde scientist team, including Wernher von Braun, intact."

Erickson calmly linked her slender hands on the table. She stared into Hollinger's blue eyes. "If this is what you desire, I will relay your information to Herr Bormann."

He stared right back. Blue eyes on blue eyes. "Do that, please."

"May we order the food now?" Erickson said. "Trapshooting always makes me hungry."

"By all means. I'm famished myself."

Thirteen

Otto Bauer fell into a deep sleep very quickly. Then, within an hour, he woke with a start. He sat up in bed. He went to the window. All was quiet. But for some strange reason the large, powerful camp lights were off. At first he assumed the generator plant had failed. Then he saw two people dressed in white crawling on their bellies towards one of the huts next to his. A machine gun glinted in the moonlight. He saw two other people. . . squatting down low.

What was this?

He was startled by a loud crash, down the hall, next to his room. Sporadic gunfire erupted, followed by footsteps. Bauer didn't know what to do, so he threw himself under the bed. Seconds later, from his vantage point on the floor, Bauer saw the door fling open and two sets of white boots.

"No one in here!"

Bauer froze. British accents. *The British were in the Antarctic!*

"Check under the bed!"

"You bet."

Bauer saw a set of boots strut over.

The sheets and mattress were flung off, exposing the bare springs. Bauer stared up through the iron mesh at two gun-bearing young men in all-white apparel.

"Get the bloody hell out of there, Kraut!"

"I'm coming," Bauer said, sheepishly.

"Ah, finally, we got one who speaks English."

Bauer rose to his feet, hands in the air. "That's correct. I do speak English, Tommy."

The soldiers grinned at the German. "A cooperative one, too, I bet."

"Nice pyjamas," one of them said, jabbing Bauer in the stomach with a gun until he winced. "Don't think I've seen flannel quite that bright a yellow."

Bauer heard gunfire outside. Some yelling.

"A present from my wife."

"If you say so. Get dressed. We're leaving."

Another jab.

"Quit it!"

"Shut up, Kraut."

"Where are you taking me?" Bauer asked.

"To our base for interrogation. Try and escape and we'll shoot you."

Bauer smiled dryly. "Are you crazy? There's no place to go."

"Yeah. And don't you forget it."

BERLIN

The teletype machine in the communications centre next door to Bormann's office began to pound away. Bormann didn't wait for Fraulein Krueger or anybody else. He got up from his desk and checked it out for himself by hunching his bulk over the machine.

Zurich.

It was in the personal code that he and Erickson had worked out. Any reference to Switzerland or any city or particular people were non-existent on the top of the page. Message finished, Bormann ripped the paper from the machine and took it to his office.

LAKE LUCERNE

Hollinger knocked on the second-floor door, two down from the elevator. Seven-fifteen was too early for him. The sun had not yet come up over the mountains.

"Come in," shouted a female voice. "It's not locked."

The American agent entered the handsomely-furnished hotel room, filled with bright wall lights. "Miss Erickson?" he called out.

A voice from the open bathroom answered, "Yes."

"Wesley Hollinger, ma'am. I got your note from the desk."

"Oh, yes. Wait a minute, won't you."

Johanna Erickson appeared, a thick towel around her body, exposing tanned arms and long, shapely legs. She was combing out her wet hair after a shower.

Hollinger was stunned. She was gorgeous, and he couldn't stop staring at her.

Her hand went to her hips. "What is the matter, Mr. Hollinger?"

"Nothing. Nothing at all. I see beautiful women wrapped in a towel, hell, almost. . . oh. . . everyday. Why should anything be the matter?"

She laughed, her dimples prominent. "I'll be right with you. I have some news. We shall have breakfast, yes?"

"Sure thing. I might be hungry."

She did not close the door completely. This surprised Hollinger.

He could see her reflection in the full-length mirror. Then, she removed her towel. She casually continued combing her hair, stark naked, as if nothing was wrong. Hollinger got a good look now. He saw everything. It had been four years since he had seen a naked woman other than Roberta. If this was 1940, when he was unattached, and footloose, he'd. . . She looked up. Her eyes were riveted on his. Or was it that. . . she. . . just happened to glance up. No, it was deliberate, or accidentally on purpose. Hollinger's heart began to stir. She knew he was looking at her. Then she shut the door closed.

He stepped forward, then hesitated, weighing it all up. *What am I doing?* he thought, suppressing an urge to push the door open on her. *Is that what she wanted, for me to come bursting in? Then what?*

"I'll wait on the couch," he called out, his voice cracking, his wife coming to mind. *What am I doing? Snap out of it, Wesley. You're not single anymore.*

Pity. I guess.

"I won't be long," she said.

The dining room was busy with customers, considering it was a Saturday and not yet eight in the morning. They were led to the same booth as the evening before. It was starting to lighten outside, through the wide, French doors overlooking the lake.

Politely waiting for Erickson to sit first, Hollinger took his seat and asked, "Why just the two of us?"

"It's the way I wish to work. I do not want all five of us to be seen together all the time. It's a precaution."

"If that's what you want. We do the same thing in our line of business."

"I know you do. Dulles is no exception." She moved closer to him, until their thighs were touching. Hollinger noticed the sweet smell of perfume on her, like a strongly scented flowerbed.

Hollinger was too embarrassed to slide away. "Dulles's name is not to be repeated, remember." And if McCreedy was right about Dulles's Nazi connections, Hollinger could see why.

"Yes, I do remember. There's another reason for the two of us to meet," she smiled, slightly.

"And what's that?"

"I think we make a handsome couple. Don't you agree?"

He couldn't drive her unclothed image from his memory. "I'm a married man, Miss Erickson."

"I know that. I saw your ring. Are you happily married?"

"Yes, I am. And my wife's expecting in May."

"Congratulations. I was married once. To a German soldier. He died on the Eastern Front."

"I'm sorry to hear that."

"I'm not."

Hollinger was taken aback. "Oh? Why is that?"

"He was a rotten man. We had divorced long before he went to war."

"Your family is German, too, isn't it?"

"German background, yes. My accent gives it away. We are German Swiss. There is a difference. My grandmother—my mother's mother—was French. I was born and schooled in Zurich."

"How did you meet your husband, if he was German?"

"I worked for a time in Berlin. Gunther came from a well-to-do family. The marriage was arranged. He was not my choice. It was many years ago. I was so young."

"You Swiss are strange people."

"Why do you say that?"

"Whose side are you on?"

"In the war?"

"No, in the World Series."

"Excuse me?"

"Never mind. Yes, I meant the war."

She pulled back. "We're on the side that wins. But we never fail to bank for anybody and everybody as we see fit. Be it British, German, Italian, American."

"But mostly the Germans. The Allied press have referred to you as the Nazi bankers."

Erickson gave him another of her dimpled smiles, followed up by a hearty laugh. "Yes, I know the saying. *Six days of the week we work for the Germans, and on the seventh day we rest and pray for the Allies.*"

"One thing's for certain. By the time the war's over, your nation in general and your family's bank in particular will undoubtedly be filthy rich."

Erickson didn't seem hurt. "I won't argue with you, Mr. Hollinger. That has been our plan. Our goal. Even so, in the midst of this war and all the calamity around us, I am a private woman of simple pleasures, such as, oh, classical music. . . champagne mixed with orange juice for breakfast. Won't you join me in my favourite liquid refreshment?" She nodded at the middle-aged waitress who had showed up at their table.

Hollinger smirked. "Well, I've never tried that before."

"Eggs? Toast? What is your fancy, Herr Hollinger?"

"I don't usually eat much for breakfast. Eggs and toast are fine, I guess. Sure."

Erickson nodded at the waitress, who seemed to know what was expected. Then she left quickly.

"Martin Bormann cabled me this morning."

"He did? Why didn't you say so earlier?"

"I wanted to get to know you a little better, away from your partner."

"Really. Well. . . what did Bormann say?"

"You'll have your blueprints."

"Question is, how soon?"

"As soon as he can have someone put them together in a package."

"What about the second part, Wernher von Braun and his team?"

"That remains to be seen. The only way you will take them in is at the end of the war. They are too valuable to the Nazi cause and too well guarded. They will stay until the end, which is not too far off."

Hollinger sighed. "So, I might be in Switzerland for a while, until all this is sorted out?"

"Yes. Maybe you might get a chance to sample other things the Swiss have to offer. We are a very hospitable people." She put her hand on his leg, above his knee, then quickly withdrew it.

Their eyes lingered.

"Do you mind forward women, Mr. Hollinger? Why, Mr. Hollinger, I do believe you're blushing."

"Look, Miss Erickson, if I didn't know any better I'd say that you're trying to seduce me," Hollinger said, staring away at Thomas McCreedy entering the dining room.

She smiled. "Mr. Hollinger, is that what you think I'm doing? Sorry, my time here is short. After breakfast, I must take my leave of you, and see you again in a few days. I will return to Zurich. I will be in touch once I hear further from Bormann."

"If he's not too busy."

"I'll see if he can tear himself away from the Fuehrer."

McCreedy walked up. "Wesley, where you been? Trying to cut a deal without me?"

Hollinger and Erickson looked up.

"Join us, Mr. McCreedy," Erickson said.

"Don't mind if I do."

Fourteen

WERRA, GERMANY—MARCH 13

The scientists found it cooler and harder to breath at six thousand feet above sea level in the alpine mountains. The air would take some getting used to.

After five disorganized days of arranging the new underground compound, Karl Zeller and Wernher von Braun eyed the flatbed truck proceeding through the gate, grinding its way into the dusty compound. An unsmiling pair of Luftwaffe guards approached the driver.

"It's a good thing we don't need a runway for it," Zeller said.

Von Braun nodded, hands in his trenchcoat pockets. "True. No room here."

"Where will we keep it hidden?"

"Under camouflage netting in the trees, right about. . . there," von Braun pointed a hundred yards across the compound.

"The best place, I suppose."

"The only place for now, Karl."

"Yes, for now," Zeller said, "until the Americans find it. We hope."

"They will. Reichsleiter Bormann, I'm sure, will lead them here personally, should he have to," von Braun said, his face fixed like stone.

"I don't doubt it. As long as he doesn't leave us out of the OSS deal."

"I thought we are part of it."

"We are," Zeller answered.

"Then quit your worrying. It's the perfect arrangement for everybody. Do as Bormann ordered you, and make a complete copy of the blueprints."

"I finished them not twenty minutes ago. That's what I came to tell you, Wernher."

"Good. The Americans must see the documents as they requested. Is the courier ready?"

"Yes."

"Then send him on his way."

"Of course, Wernher." Zeller turned to leave.

"Oh, Karl. I have some bad news." Von Braun faced his friend. "Goering telephoned me. We have lost communications with Camp Berlin."

"We have?"

"Their last transmission was garbled, but spoke something about a British attack. You know what this means?"

Zeller paused to think it through. "Yes. Our titanium supply has been cut off."

"We only had enough shipped to us for one fighter. This"—he pointed to the truck—"is the only one of its kind."

"Then we had better treat it nicely."

"To be sure, Karl. To be sure."

NORTHEAST GERMANY

An intoxicated Hermann Goering stood dejected in the hall of his empty country estate overlooking the brilliant view of the bluff and tranquil waters of the Dolln See. Alone, he looked around, slowly, his footsteps echoing off the bare timber walls of Karinhall. This was Goering's getaway, named after Karin, his first wife, a gentle, blonde, elegant Swede. A lavish, thatched-roof country lodge, Karinhall was built in Norse style on Schorf Heath, a rocky Prussian terrain of lake and forest reaching from northeast of Berlin to the Baltic coast. At a cost of fifteen million Reich marks out of the pockets of hard-working German taxpayers, Karinhall had the best of everything, presented dramatically by Goering, who prided himself on his Renaissance possessions. In her heyday, the estate had Flemish tapestries, fountains, statues, crystal chandeliers, expensive sculptures and embroidery, and a full load of stolen art treasures from occupied countries.

But this was no more.

Today, the estate was empty. Everything had been shipped south, close to Switzerland for safety. Just minutes ago, Goering had heard the exact count given to him by his aides—739 paintings, sixty pieces of sculptures, and fifty tapestries. They were now being shipped to the Party Chancellery in Berlin. From there they would be sent south in a truck that would leave Berlin tomorrow—March 14.

The Reichmarshall considered his bleak future. He had a copy of the V-4 blueprints under his shirt, should he need them. His red sash and his medallion had been carefully packed away in a hidden compartment in his suitcase. He suddenly brought the Order and Bormann to mind. The Reichsleiter had said that the Americans—the OSS—had made contact with Bormann's banker in Switzerland. But could that runt-of-the-litter-kiss-ass Bormann really be trusted? Could anyone in Germany be trusted? That afternoon, before the phone lines were cut, Hitler telephoned to order that every captured Allied bomber crew be turned over to the Gestapo and shot. Had the Fuehrer flipped his lid?

Goering turned his back to the Dolln See beyond, and shuffled out of the estate through the huge wooden door, head slightly down, tears in his bloodshot eyes. His hands could not stop shaking. He finally stuffed them in the pockets of his Luftwaffe greatcoat. His knew his condition was serious and worsening. He was a man on the edge. He met his chauffeur outside. The sweet smell of pine seemed to revive him. Spring was in the air. The temperature had been rising steadily that week.

"All is ready for your departure, Herr Reichmarshall."

"Thank you, William."

Goering saw that everything was in order. Hundreds of erect Luftwaffe troops were standing guard in a circle around the estate. The passenger door was open to his armour-plated limousine. Beside another automobile, his manservant, Robert, and nurse, Christa, in charge of the drug and medicine cabinet, along with his doctor, Ramon von Ondarza, waited respectfully for the Luftwaffe Commander-in-Chief whose once-lethal Luftwaffe was now in shambles.

Goering took one last, long, inebriated look at his beloved lodge and squeezed into the limousine. *How could this have happened?*

Fifteen

It was a bright day. Few clouds. Perfect visibility. Too bad he was in the midst of the stiffest anti-aircraft fire in all his twenty missions. The flak officer at the briefing that morning knew what he was talking about when he said that Berlin had the heaviest guns of the German cities.

Sergeant Art Tooney spun his ball turret back and forth. The bomb doors opened with a creak. He could clearly see the other bombers in the huge stream of hundreds, arranged in V's, flights, squadrons, and groups. They were a solid overcast of bombers. Another Maximum Effort. Flanking the bombers, far out to the left and right, dots in the sky, were the escorting P-47 and P-51 fighters. He looked down and saw the streets in the Berlin suburbs over 20,000 feet below. He closed his eyes, wishing it was over. He swallowed hard. Then. . . one explosion shook *Lucky Lady*, belting him to the side.

Another explosion rocked the bomber.

That was close. Too close.

Tooney opened his eyes. A B-17 in the formation was going down, two engines smoking, tail plane shot away! White smoke meant loss of oil. One chute. . . two. . . Then another bomber took a hit. Black smoke this time. A fire. And then a third in the group to the rear, a giant dark hole in her fuselage. She was falling out of formation. Tooney swallowed, on the verge of vomiting. Panic infected him, then passed quickly. . . as if he had been slapped in the face. *That's not going to happen to us! Not us. We're the lead ship of the mid-group. Hang in there, or she's goodbye, Charlie.*

Tension was the killer for Tooney. Staying alert, constantly searching the sky, was too much sometimes. On this mission, his oxygen mask had iced up, and his heated flying suit was not operating properly. Either it was too hot or too cold. Now it was too hot on the gloves, and was burning his fingers. Damn! It was not his day.

Over the intercom he could hear the bombardier instruct the pilot on the bomb run. "STEADY. . . STEADY. . . LEFT A BIT."

Then the bomber shook violently.

"WHAT WAS THAT?" asked a voice.

"WE'VE BEEN HIT! NAVIGATOR TO PILOT. NUMBER TWO ENGINE ON FIRE!"

Tooney felt the bomber losing altitude. Oh no! Shit, no! Still, they remained on their bomb run.

"I SEE IT. RELAX. I'M SHUTTING IT DOWN. BOMBARDIER, HOW IS THAT TARGET?"

"I HAVE IT IN MY SIGHTS."

"TELL ME WHEN. MAKE IT QUICK."

"BAD CROSSWIND, SKIPPER."

"CAN'T HELP IT."

A long pause. . .

"NOW!"

"IT'S ALL YOURS. YOU HAVE THE AIRCRAFT."

Tooney knew what was happening. On every bomb run, the bombardier, once he had the target through his eyepiece, would ask for control of the aircraft. In essence, he was flying the bomber, although only for a short time, until he dropped the payload. The plane had to stay level, unable to dodge the flak.

Another long pause. . . an eternity to Tooney. . . waiting for those magic words from the navigator.

"BOMBS GONE! LET'S GET OUTTA HERE!"

Tooney felt *Lucky Lady* jerk upwards, free of four-thousand-pounds of explosives. He stared below to watch the bombs descend. Part-way down, they meshed in with the other bombs from the formation. Then. . . he saw the flashing rings of destruction as each bomb collided with the earth. One. . . two. . . three. . . Within seconds, too many, too fast to count. Dark, billowing smoke began to rise. By the time the formation banked left to return to England, Tooney wondered what it was like for someone caught in the midst of all that hell on earth down below.

It took most of the week to get the package together that Erickson had promised. McCreedy and Hollinger studied the blueprints and miscellaneous folders relating to the German secret weapons at a round table in Hollinger's room, while Johanna Erickson looked on. Before their eyes were the diagrams and formulas for missiles of short-range and long-range variety, new jet fighters, revolutionary hand weapons called lasers, drawings of night-vision goggles. . . there was no end to it. Hollinger was especially fascinated by the V-2, the supersonic rocket that had been devastating parts of London.

"What do you say now, Mr. Hollinger?" she said, standing over them.

Hollinger was speechless.

"We're impressed, to say the least, by the weaponry," McCreedy said in his Virginian drawl, adjusting his glasses.

Erickson folded her arms over her white, silk blouse. She was smartly-dressed in business attire, black skirt and matching jacket. "I thought so."

"We didn't realize that the Germans were this advanced," Hollinger said, finding his tongue, holding some of the files. "Not by a long shot. These concentration camp photos are most disturbing." He saw scrawny prisoners with pathetic faces, dressed in mere rags, peering through a barbwire fence. "You say Heinrich Himmler is responsible for this?"

"According to Bormann's sources, yes."

"Jews?"

"Yes. An elimination of a race is what it is. "

"Awful. There's going to be hell to pay for this."

"Do we still have a deal?"

"Yes," Hollinger replied, glancing at McCreedy beside him, "except for one, tiny little detail."

"That is?" Erickson wondered.

"There's no paperwork for the Foo Fighter."

"The which?"

Hollinger stood to face the pretty Erickson. They locked eyes. "The Foo Fighter."

"Never heard of it," she said.

"We have. Why isn't it in here?"

"I don't know. I repeat, I've never heard of it."

"Tell Bormann we're not talking unless we include the Foo Fighter."

Erickson sighed, heavily. "I will. But he won't like it. You must consider one thing. It is very risky to send more paperwork through the lines, if there is such a machine as this Foo Fighter."

"There is."

"Very risky. It could fall into the wrong hands. We've been getting away with it so far, but—"

"Then tell Bormann to think of something, because we *want* the Foo Fighter."

Over Germany

If it wasn't for the escorting P-51 fighter, Tooney's crew would be in terrible trouble. Over enemy territory, with one engine out, prop feathered, the bomber pilot was doing all he could to keep *Lucky Lady* at 10,000 feet. But it was no use. They were still ten minutes from the German coast, and the North Sea.

The cloud was increasing now. Tooney looked over at the P-51 pilot easing alongside the bomber, twenty yards to port. Tooney waved. The pilot waved back, thumbs up. Tooney turned the turret aft. Suddenly. . . blasting out of the clouds came one of those weird fighters again. Tooney got a good look at it this time, as it flew by on a parallel course. Tooney warned his pilot over the intercom and cocked his guns, bearing down on the target. He got away some shots, but they went wild.

The P-51 pilot broke off and gave chase.

Now there were more of the weird fighters. Two. . . three. . . four. . .

Tooney stabbed at his intercom switch. "BALL GUNNER TO PILOT!"

"WHAT IS IT?" answered the voice of discipline.

"FOO FIGHTERS, SIR. FOUR OF THEM THIS TIME. SIX O'CLOCK LEVEL."

Tooney watched in horror as one of them tucked in close and fired something resembling a red beam at one of the starboard engines. Then it broke off.

"NUMBER ONE ENGINE ON FIRE," the pilot said, calmly.

"NORTH SEA BELOW, SIR," announced the navigator.

Tooney felt the stricken aircraft nosing down even more steeply. He whirred completely around in his turret. The Foo Fighters were gone as quickly as they had arrived on the scene!

Thank God!

"PILOT TO CREW. WE HAVE TO JETTISON EVERYTHING WE CAN. PILOT TO BALL GUNNER. GET OUT OF YOUR TURRET, SERGEANT. RIGHT NOW!"

"GOT YOU, SKIPPER." Tooney unhooked his oxygen and heater wires and turned the ball down to line up the turret with the opening to the mid-section of the aircraft. The door cranked open, and there to help Tooney out was the left-waist gunner, the right-waist gunner standing alongside.

Tooney looked around at the grim faces of the gunners. "Where's Henderson?" he asked them, making a move towards the aft section.

He was stopped by a stiff hand on the shoulder. "I wouldn't go back there, if I were you," said the left gunner.

"Why not?"

"Because. . . because. . . Henderson bought it," the right gunner answered.

"How? When?"

"On the bomb run. Flak blew his head off."

"Shit!" Tooney gulped. "Let's get to work, I guess."

The crew shed everything they could out the hatches—guns, ammunition, sidearms, flak suits. And they still were losing altitude. The co-pilot scrambled to the waist-section, and met up with the gunners. The slipstream blasted by the two open waist windows. "The skipper wants us to get rid of the ball!" he yelled to be heard.

The gunners looked at each other, numbed.

"Do it!" the co-pilot screamed at them. "I'll help. Where do you keep the tool kit?"

The right-waist gunner unclipped the wrenches from the side of the fuselage. They started the process by loosening the four large bolts on the ball. They took turns, five of them. It was exhausting work. Pulling the bolts off, they removed the ring gear, then knocked off the four safety hangars. They all breathed a sigh. But there was more to go—twelve small bolts, three in each corner.

"Move it!" the co-pilot blared, assisting the men. "We're still in a dive!"

They continued to work quickly and methodically, trying not to think of the gradual, yet dangerous descent of the bomber. When the last bolt popped off, twenty minutes after starting the whole procedure, the men stared in disbelief. The ball should have just fallen free, but didn't.

"Jump on it!" Tooney said.

"*Yeah*, you jump on it!" the tail gunner answered.

"OK, I will. But you guys hang onto me, just in case I slip through."

"Right."

The two waist gunners grabbed Tooney as he banged down twice on the ball with his boots.

Nothing happened.

"Again," said the co-pilot.

Tooney jumped once more.

This time the turret let go with a giant whoosh! The men tumbled backwards. Then, one at a time, they eased forward to the gigantic hole to watch the one-thousand-pound-plus ball turret head to the water.

There it goes, thought Tooney. *My best seat in the house.*

"We did it!" the co-pilot screamed, looking around, the slipstream thundering through the new space. "Hey, I think we're levelling off! We're going to make it!"

Sixteen

Colonel Lampert dialled the number for Churchill's War Room at 10 Downing Street.

"Sir, it's Lampert."

"Yes, colonel," Churchill answered, gruffly.

"We have some startling results from our Antarctic interrogation of the German scientists. Our truth drug did the job again."

"What did you find?"

Lampert sucked on his unlit pipe. "The Germans had been there for a year, almost right under our noses. They were mining through the ice and snow."

"Mining? Mining what?"

"Different minerals. Oil, lead, zinc, and. . . titanium," Lampert said, emphasizing the last mineral.

"I'm not familiar with titanium."

"Most people aren't. It's rare. It's light, strong, and resistant to high temperature. A load of it had already been shipped out by Condor before we caught up with them."

"How did the scientists get there in the first place?"

"U-Boats. Here's where the story gets interesting. Our boys captured a German submarine, U-344, off the coast while it was refuelling."

"Refuelling!"

"We interrogated them, too. The Germans, it seems, have been mapping out territory on the continent, the northern part, a place they call Neuschwabenland. A few hundred miles to the east of the

119

mining expedition, by the way. There is said to be a deep subsea trench that runs completely *under* the Antarctic."

"Under? Did you say under?"

"Yes, sir. The U-Boats have been using it for four years. Our men are investigating more of this now. This trench is also said to have caves, warm water lakes, and is supposed to be suitable for human habitation. We have compiled some wild stories of subs heading south to this Neuschwabenland, under the continent and coming out south of New Zealand. "

"Could this passage be a future Nazi hideout?"

"With the war coming to a close, it's not out of the question, sir. That's not all. We have found the existence of a secret Nazi society who refer to themselves as the Order of the Knights of National Socialism, to which the U-Boat skipper and one of the scientists belong."

"Who heads it up?"

"No one seems to know who it is, sir. We have, however, found a copy of their oath aboard the U-Boat. They do refer to a Commander Fuehrer and his divine wisdom. It could be their version of God. . ."

"Or Hitler. Interesting. No, what am I saying. It's shocking!"

"I quite agree."

"I smell an escape route of sorts."

"So do I. This trench, sir, should we investigate it further? If so, we're looking at involving the Royal Navy."

There was a long pause on the prime minister's line. "Keep it within the MI-6 for the time being. But I will order a Navy patrol off the coast of this. . . what do you call it?"

"Neuschwabenland, sir."

The Rhine River — March 21

General George Patton's U.S. Third Army had finally reached the Rhine. The afternoon air was still and cool. There was no enemy activity on the far bank. Patton jumped down from his command jeep and proceeded to urinate in the river. His men laughed. The general had kept his promise to take a leak in the Rhine River as soon as he had come upon it.

"I enjoyed that. Now, back to work," Patton chuckled, zipping himself up and glancing across the river that separated liberated France from Hitler's Germany. He turned to his XII Corps subordinate, bespectacled

General Manton Eddy and ordered, "We've got to establish a bridge-head at once!"

"Yes, sir."

Patton had been crystallizing a plan in his mind for weeks. He would be the first Allied commander to cross into Hitler's Fatherland, and thus spoil British General Bernard Montgomery's long-anticipated March 23rd crossing of the Rhine, amid press releases and such. Although Patton had not received prior permission to cross from Supreme Commander Eisenhower, he would instead get his men over the river, where they would be engaged by the enemy and forced to hold their ground and not turn back. The British and Montgomery would have to take a back seat to the Third Army.

Eddy and Patton hunched over a map on Patton's jeep. "We'll cross here, tomorrow night," Patton said, pointing a steady finger near the town of Mainz.

"Yes, sir."

Patton grinned wide. He could see the whole central belly of Germany opening up to his tanks.

Lake Lucerne

Wesley Hollinger was bored batty, as he put it to McCreedy twice, waiting the whole week for word from Bormann's contact. At 10pm on the fifth day, the American answered his hotel room door to find Johanna Erickson standing outside.

"Look who's here."

"Surprised?"

"Not really," Hollinger answered. "You did say you were returning."

"I did, didn't I? Do you want to go for a walk? I have a favourite scenic spot by the lake that's quite breath-taking."

"Why not tell me what you have to right here? Let's go out to the balcony."

She smiled. "I might be convinced."

What was she up to? Hollinger thought. "Would you like a drink? Schnapps? Wine?"

"Schnapps will be fine."

"I'll have one, too. Go on out, please, I'll be right with you."

Through the French doors, they could see that the moon was up. A

121

pleasant evening to sit out. The temperature was near sixty. The sun had set an hour ago. Hollinger went to a cupboard in the hallway to pour the drinks. Erickson followed him, shutting the hall light switch off. He turned around at the sound of her steps. She moved closer with her easy grace, not making a sound.

"What is it, Miss Erickson?"

"I have a message for you." She backed him into the wall, and put her arms over his broad, strong shoulders. Their faces were inches apart. "From Martin Bormann."

Caught off guard, Hollinger was aroused by this exotic woman's forwardness and her perfume smell of spring flowers. "What's the message?"

"Just a moment." She kissed him boldly on the lips.

He couldn't help it. Her beauty, her delightful dimples, the smell of her perfume, was all too much. His hands seized her slim waist like magic. He found it hard to breath, and it had nothing to do with the mountain air. He pulled her close, stroking her smooth hair. They covered each other with passionate kisses. She was the first to break off. "Bormann can't deliver till the war's over. But I can deliver now." She kissed him again, this time finding every corner of his mouth.

They continued kissing, uninhibited. Hollinger gripped her harder until their bodies were pressed together. He had no intention of putting a halt to this. In a flash, his bachelor days came back to him. He was single all over again. She stood back and undid the top three buttons of her blouse as he watched. She took Hollinger's right hand, and led it slowly, deliberately, inside. She wasn't wearing a bra. His heart beat faster. He knew that from this point on, there was one logical conclusion to this. Bed.

"You never did tell me whether you like forward women," she whispered.

Then he thought of Roberta, and found himself torn between the two. He removed his hand. "Wait!"

"What's the matter, Wesley? Don't quit now," she said softly.

"Wait, I said. Who do you think you are? I know why you came back." He shook her. "You're not going to get away with it!"

"Stop it! You're hurting me."

"Who do you think you are? Bormann's whore?" He pushed her away, harder than he had wanted to. She crashed into the wall. He looked down at her, poker-faced. "It's Bormann, isn't it! Isn't it! What did he promise you? Money? What?"

She tried to get up. "You are very foolish, Wesley Hollinger." She got to her feet and buttoned her blouse, her nostrils flaring.

Hollinger folded his arms. "Tell Bormann that I want those damn Foo Fighter blueprints. No more games. Not from you or anybody else. And by the way, I don't like forward women. Especially women who try to use me."

They were silent a long time, both reluctant to utter the next word, both catching their breaths. She squared her shoulders, then left without a word, slamming the door behind her.

"What's the matter?" Hollinger said to himself, his face warm and red. "No goodbye?"

Seventeen

Bormann and Goering walked and listened to the distant thump of the artillery shells far to the east, and tried to show no fear of the Russian General Zhukov who was closing in on Berlin.

"Your banker didn't take care of it, obviously," Goering barked, swinging his baton by his side in the Chancellery garden.

"No," Bormann answered stiffly, dragging on his cigarette, picturing Johanna Erickson. He didn't want to be reminded of his misfortune. Too bad, she had always gotten the job done before.

"What now?"

"Consider our alternatives, Herr Goering. The courier line is far too dangerous with the advancing Allies approaching us. Patton has already crossed the Rhine and is heading towards the Thuringia underground factory. We know that the British have overrun Camp Berlin. We have only one choice." Bormann slowed his steps and looked across at the Reichmarshall.

"What's that?"

"It's crazy, but it's our only solution."

"What? Tell me."

Bormann groped for the words. "Let the Americans see this Foo Fighter, as they call it."

They stopped.

"How can we do that?"

"Bring them into Germany to see the V-4 with their own eyes. To show that we are acting in good faith."

"You have to be out of your mind!"

"I've never been more rational," Bormann answered, as calmly as he could.

"How do you propose we pull this off?"

"Fly them in."

"What!"

"You have the authority to provide free access into Germany by air, providing the plane has Swiss markings."

"Yes, I have the authority as Luftwaffe leader, technically, but—"

"But what?"

"How will the Americans get past Himmler's SS, who are guarding the entrance to the compound?"

"I have a source."

"Who?" Goering wanted to know.

"One of the scientists, who is allowed as much free movement about the country as von Braun. He will meet with them and get them past the compound on written orders from the Fuehrer. I will see to the paperwork."

"Who is this scientist?"

"Karl Zeller."

"I know who you mean. So he's the one who's been feeding you information all this time?"

"Yes," Bormann admitted.

"Oh, it doesn't matter now."

"No, it doesn't. He's trustworthy. He's on our side." Bormann puffed on his cigarette. "Well, can you do it?"

Goering twirled his baton. "I. . . yes, I suppose. The whole thing seems crazy to me. If anyone finds out about our little escapade, we are dead, Bormann."

Hitler's secretary smiled through his cigarette smoke. "Drastic times spawn drastic measures. To tell you the truth, it seems crazy to me, too. But what else can we do?"

"Himmler could be the problem."

"He'll never know."

"How do you know that he doesn't already?"

It was dawn when they boarded the C-47 with the red-and-white Swiss flag markings parked on the field in the clearing. Hollinger had qualms about this bizarre mission. Was this a cruel April Fool's joke for him and McCreedy, flying into Germany under Swiss diplomatic cover? Standing stiffly inside the metal fuselage, arms folded, was Johanna Erickson, in black slacks and white blouse. She led the Americans down the fuselage, pointing to a set of seats facing each other on the starboard side.

She reached into her briefcase and handed the agents the necessary documents. "Here are your passports," she began, as the three sat. "Mr. Hollinger, you are Frederick Kleeg. Mr. McCreedy, your name is Jacob Spitteler. You are officials of the Swiss Red Cross. Your knowledge of the German language will benefit you both, I'm sure. Any questions?"

"Yeah, I still don't get something, Miss Erickson," Hollinger asked. "Am I to understand that we, as Red Cross representatives, will be observing prisoner working conditions of a top secret military project?"

"Yes."

"Hell! Isn't this a terrible breach of security on the Germans' part?"

"Bormann and the others want to save their necks. Earlier in the war, or even a few months ago, this never would have been considered. From what I understand, the Germans only have one Foo Fighter prototype, which they will try to hide, but not that hard—just enough for you to be able to see it. Inside the caves, separate components for it are being constructed. We will be met and escorted through the compound by one of the scientists, Karl Zeller, an assistant to Wernher von Braun."

"Von Braun, huh," Hollinger said, excited, blinking at her.

"However, he will be away during our visit, I'm told to tell you, taking care of some V-2 matters."

"Too bad, I wish I could meet him."

"Zeller will also hand over the Foo Fighter blueprints. I should point out that they refer to the fighter as the V-4."

"OK. Got you. But I thought prisoners in war time weren't supposed to be put to work?"

"That's why we're there to see if the rumours are true. The Germans will undoubtedly clear the caves of the prisoners before we get there and replace them with healthy Germans."

"Clever. Then switch back once we've left."

"Yes."

"I thought so."

She produced a wide map, and opened it up in their laps. "We are here, fifteen kilometres from the German border. Our flight path will take us over Bavaria, three hundred and fifty kilometres to Werra, in the Thuringia Mountains. We have been promised access by Hermann Goering himself, as long as we remain in the specified corridor."

"Then Goering must be an accomplice of Bormann?" McCreedy asked Erickson, glancing at Hollinger. "How about that."

"I don't know, and I don't care."

One engine on the C-47 whirred, cranked, and caught fire. Erickson didn't move. Number two engine started.

"You wouldn't, by chance, be coming with us?" McCreedy asked.

"Yes, of course," she said, nodding, eyeing Hollinger. "This is part of my business transaction. Nothing else. Furthermore, I don't want you two to foul up. Incidentally, I'll be using my own name. I'm leading this Red Cross team of ours."

Hollinger smirked, the aircraft fuselage vibrating from the engines. "Fine with me... I mean... us."

"By the way," McCreedy spoke up, "how do we know the Germans won't hold us for ransom? We're at war with these people."

"That's not likely. What's more, they are losing, Mr. McCreedy. What's the point of holding two Americans and a Swiss banker for ransom at this time? It's going to be a long flight, so relax and get comfortable, Mr. Kleeg and Mr. Spitteler," Erickson said, looking out the window, forcing an ending to the briefing.

The C-47 turned left sharply. It began to move and bounce slowly across the grass field, until it gathered speed. As the aircraft took to the air in a flat climb, Hollinger's stomach remained on the ground. Why did he get himself into these predicaments?

Eighteen

The C-47 banked over the gravel airfield inside the mountain valley before it touched down with a heavy thud.

"You're looking a little green there buddy," McCreedy said to Hollinger, sitting in the seat across the aisle, as the aircraft bounced along. "You all right?"

"No. I hate flying," Hollinger replied, glad he was at the end of the bumpy ride into enemy territory. Twice along the way, ME-109s had nudged in close, then backed off. It was unnerving. Coming down the fuselage ramp, the company of three saw a dusty, black Mercedes waiting one hundred feet ahead. A lone occupant stepped forward to greet them as they drew near.

"Welcome to _Projekt Equinox_," the man said in German. "I am Karl Zeller, assistant to Wernher von Braun." With a smile, he stared at Johanna Erickson. "This is a pleasure, Miss Erickson. I didn't expect someone so pretty."

Erickson held out her hand. "You are too kind. These are my _associates_."

Zeller studied the two men as if they were under a microscope. "You are the Americans?"

"Yes," Hollinger answered for the two.

"You look ill," Zeller said to Hollinger.

"It's nothing."

"Quickly, in the auto. We are only seven kilometres from the site."

Once inside the Mercedes, Zeller nervously drove off. "It is cool today."

Erickson agreed. "Yes, it is."

"I have the documents on my person, signed by the Fuehrer to allow you access to the compound as Swiss Red Cross representatives."

"How did you manage that?" McCreedy asked. "Especially with Patton's Third Army so close?"

"That is none of your business. Concentrate on your mission."

"Dual mission," said Hollinger.

"Yes, your dual mission, Mr–?"

"I go by the name of Frederick Kleeg," said Hollinger.

"I urge the three of you to stay with me at all times. Do not wander off. Do not ask anybody else questions. Observe only. Speak only when spoken to. Am I clear on this?"

The three nodded.

"Will we be able to observe your V-4?" Hollinger asked, bluntly.

"We will give you the greatest of opportunities to see it."

"You mean we might not?"

"You will have to be most indiscreet."

The Mercedes stopped at the gate. Zeller got out. "Stay here," he ordered the others through the open window. Then he went inside. The huge metal gate slammed behind him.

Hollinger saw the men in SS uniforms beyond the wire compound. "The SS! This better work," he said to the others.

"Yes, the SS. But they are not allowed on the inside. Only Luftwaffe guards can do that. Please be quiet!" Erickson warned. "Here comes a guard."

An SS soldier, carrying a machine gun, walked up to the car's front bumper, and looked beyond the windshield to the occupants. Zeller returned with an SS officer.

"These are the Swiss Red Cross people?" the officer asked firmly, by the side of the vehicle.

"Yes, Herr Colonel."

"You are responsible for them."

Zeller nodded. "Yes, sir. I realize that, Herr Colonel."

"Let's see them out here. Quickly."

"Of course."

Zeller motioned to his company. Erickson got out first, followed by

Hollinger, then McCreedy. The officer looked them over. After what seemed like an eternity, he gestured to the guard to open the gate. As the first three passed, he stopped Hollinger with a hand on the chest. "What is your name?" in said stiffly, in German.

"Frederick Kleeg," Hollinger said, as calmly as he could.

"Good luck," the colonel blurted in English.

Hollinger's nerves tingled. He almost answered in English. Instead, he caught himself and looked at the colonel as if he did not understand.

"Proceed," the colonel said, in German. He watched the group walk into the compound, then he headed off in the opposite direction. At his small, clapboard office, he dialled the desk telephone.

"Let me speak to the Reichsfuehrer, please."

"Who is this?"

"Colonel Geinns."

"Just a moment."

A short wait.

"Yes, colonel."

"Herr Reichsfuehrer, the Red Cross officials have arrived."

"And?"

"Two of them don't look Swiss to me."

"What do they look like to you?"

"I'm sure that one of them is an American."

"I see. Keep it to yourself."

"But Herr Reichsfuehrer. An *American*. . . here?

"Never mind."

"What do you want me to do?"

"Absolutely nothing. Goodbye."

Geinns stared at the receiver in his hands. Americans on the compound and he was to do nothing? Had the whole world gone mad?

Hollinger was all eyes, glancing, staring, observing, everywhere at once, before his attention turned to the camouflage netting in the trees. Zeller caught up to Hollinger, walked alongside, as the group slowly made their way to the tunnel.

"Ah, Mr. Kleeg, you saw it."

Hollinger looked away, trying to remember what the B-17 ball gunner and the other airmen had described during the Foo File interviews.

From what he could recall, they were dead right. It did appear to be a plate, from what he could see of the half-covered machine, only the metal bottom and undercarriage exposed. A flat, shiny plate, at that.

They arrived at the cave entrance, stopped and turned around. Their view of the V-4 outside was obstructed by a line of trees. They heard drilling behind them, on the other side of a canvas wall.

"Now, let me show you an assembly line that you might find interesting. Remember, you are to observe the prisoner conditions. Nothing else."

"Wait, tell me about your fighter," Hollinger asked. "Before we go in."

"Then you are fascinated with our little magnetohyrodynamic propulsion device."

"Ah. . . yes. Whatever."

"What do you want? Technical matter?"

"Yes, anything. How does it turn? Does it have ailerons?"

"Indeed, it does."

"What's it made of?"

"Titanium. With some magnesium. It's computer-operative, including the navigation. Nothing to do with what you Americans and British call *seat-of-the-pants flying*. It is aerodynamically sound. The wings and rudder are integrated into the body. Perfect three hundred and sixty degree visibility from the cockpit."

"I'll say. What's the size of it?" Hollinger pulled out a notepad.

"Diameter is forty meters. Base to canopy height is thirty-two meters."

Hollinger jotted down the figures. "What kind of powerplant do you use?"

"Liquid air turbojet."

"Weapons?"

"Missiles, guns, and lasers."

"Lasers!"

"Yes, a concentrated path of heat that will, in the future, make bullets obsolete. Some have nicknamed it a death ray. We are also working on the V-4 being invisible to radar."

"Go on!" McCreedy said.

"It's true."

"If the leading edges are thin enough, it will be."

"But if it's too thin, won't it fall apart?" asked Hollinger.

Zeller shook his head. "Not with titanium."

"Geez! Where did you come up with all these discoveries?"

"We caught the rest of the world napping. That's not all. If we had the time—but we won't because of this war—we could determine how our V-4 could ride the wave of anti-gravity."

"What are you talking about?"

"The earth has an electromagnetic field. Break into it, and a whole new world of propulsion is possible, without fuel and engines, where speeds many times the speed of sound are within one's grasp."

"Sounds nutty to me. Anyway, I'm sure everything will be covered in your paperwork?"

"What paperwork?"

"The blueprints and all that of the Foo Fighter, I mean the V-4."

"All you get is a look."

Hollinger grunted. "Who said?"

"Martin Bormann. You don't get your blueprints or anything else until he is safely out of the country."

"Wait a damn minute, here! We're tired of this run around. You're in no position to dictate terms. Patton is only a few days away from overrunning this place."

"On the contrary. We are in the best of positions. Do as we say or we will blow up every trace of every secret weapon across Germany, including the V-4."

"You wouldn't."

"It's up to you."

Hollinger and McCreedy glanced at each other. They had no choice.

Zeller walked over to the canvas, and flipped it back. Thirty feet away was the first of the smaller versions of the V-4. "Here they are. The radio-controlled models. The Messerschmitt V-4 Experimental Series 1-1a. After you. The lady first."

Nineteen

Bormann lifted the receiver late in the evening. It was raining in the German capital.

"Herr Reichsleiter, it is I, Zeller."

"Just a moment." Bormann shut the door to his office. "Yes, what is it?"

"Is our telephone line tapped?"

"Of course not. What do you want?"

"The Americans have come and gone, Herr Reichsleiter. They saw their Foo Fighter. They will negotiate now. We have them where we want them."

"Good. I'm delighted. The terms?"

"They want the V-4 prototype, our scientist team, including von Braun, and everything else pertaining to secret weapons that they can get their hands on."

"Yes, that's fine. I expected that. Go on."

"They agree to the V-4 blueprints later on, once you are out of the country. They didn't like our change of plans."

"Too damn bad for them, Zeller."

"You, Herr Reichsleiter, will be given free access through Switzerland upon your escape from Berlin. A tentative route has been worked out that will see you safely through American lines."

"Excellent. I agree. Listen to me. Hide the V-4 prototype under anything, camouflage netting, cut-down trees, whatever you can find. Take all the paperwork out of there. Then, blow up the radio-controlled models."

135

"Did I hear you correctly? Blow them up!"

"Yes, that's what I said. Patton is coming your way, you fool! I will get the Fuehrer to sign the orders for the Luftwaffe to destroy the models." Bormann lowered his voice. "In his state, he will sign anything right now. He trusts me explicitly."

"Yes, of course, Herr Reichsleiter. I will do as you say. Where shall we go?"

"There's an abandoned resort near Bleicherode in the Harz Mountains. Stay there."

"Will that be another Fuehrer order?"

"Yes. Anything else?"

"No, Herr Reichsleiter."

"Goodbye."

Bormann smiled, placing the receiver in the cradle. Good news. The best news in weeks. The Americans badly wanted the V-4 blueprints. The Reichsleiter returned to his letter writing, his mind flashing back to his wife at their comfortable house in the Bavarian mountains near the Swiss border.

My Gerda darling,

We must never cease to rejoice that we have our Fuehrer, for our unshakeable faith in ultimate victory is founded in a very large measure on the fact that he exists—on his genius and rocklike determination. I have no premonition of death; on the contrary, my burning desire is to live.

Keep well

BERN—APRIL 2

Switzerland's OSS director Allen Dulles was fascinated by the blueprints McCreedy and Hollinger had brought back. One paper in particular held his attention.

"Delta-wing fighters, are they?"

"Yes, sir." Hollinger leaned over the office desk. "That is the Horten HO-IX. They call them swept-back wings. That model has two jet engines capable of 2,000 pounds of thrust each."

"It appears to be a flying wing."

"It sure does."

"What's thrust? Never heard of it."

"A new term for the jet era. Rather like a horsepower rating."

"How much exactly is two thousand pounds of thrust?"

"A lot," answered McCreedy, when Hollinger failed to find the words.

"What kind of speeds are we talking about?"

"Faster than the speed of sound, sir," Hollinger replied.

Dulles stared at them. "What else?" He flipped to the next sheet, a strange-looking vertical-standing craft, shaped like a torpedo. He read the pencilled-in name in the corner of the paper. "Focke-Wulf Trieb-flugel. Reminds me of one of those things experimented with in the States. A helicopter."

"And what is this?"

"The HS-293, the world's first air-to-ground guided missile with a one-thousand-pound warhead."

Dulles pulled out another sheet. "And this?"

Hollinger smiled. "Another German first. That, sir, is a rocket that in tests going back to 1942, can be fired from a submerged U-boat."

Dulles shook his head, and flipped through several more papers, the 163 Komet, the 262 jet, the V-1 Flying Bomb, until he came to the V-2 rocket, which he studied for several moments. Then he pushed the blueprints to the side of his desk. "I never would have believed it had I not seen these."

"Us neither, sir." McCreedy replied.

Hollinger folded his arms. "And we saw the Foo Fighter, the pilot-operated one, and the radio-controlled models manufactured underground."

"But no paperwork for our people?"

"No, sir. That was part of the deal we cut. They're holding out. We get it once Bormann is safely out of Germany and on his way to South America."

Dulles removed his glasses and rubbed his eyes. "Good work nonetheless. I will contact Donovan in Washington. And I will have copies made for him and Dorwin."

"Sir," Hollinger said. "The German underground facility is amazing. I don't know how they do it. Tunnels everywhere. Machine shops, launch pads, assembly lines, and living quarters."

"Astounding. By the way, I just got word before you two arrived. Patton is within striking distance of that factory you were at near Werra. So stick around, Mr. Hollinger. This isn't over with yet. One other thing, did you have any problems in Germany?"

Hollinger smiled. "Us? No problems at all. Piece of cake."

Hollinger took the stairs, and turned a corner to the front lobby. There she was, holding a briefcase.

"Johanna Erickson! What are you doing here?"

She was dressed exquisitely, brown skirt, white silk blouse that showed off her figure, and she smelled of spring flowers. "I was on my way to the office. I heard you were in town."

"How did you know?"

"I have my ways."

"Yeah, I can imagine."

She looked around. No one within earshot. "I came to pass on Bormann's final message. The V-4 prototype will be spared. Hidden. Some of the radio models will be blown up to appear that they all were destroyed."

"Why?"

"Because the SS—Heinrich Himmler—is still technically in charge of security outside the compound."

"I know that. So, what of it?"

"Something has to be done to put on a big enough show to the other Germans, including Himmler."

"And the files?"

"Safely put away by a member of von Braun's staff. You find von Braun, you find the files."

"Another waiting game."

"It won't be too long. The Third Reich is finished. Also, I came to say goodbye. My involvement in this has come to an end. With the war drawing to a close, you can deal directly with Bormann and the scientists. OK, Yank?"

Hollinger took a long time to answer. "Yeah."

She held out her hand. "No bad feelings."

He didn't budge. If she wasn't so beautiful, she'd be pathetic. "I'm a one-woman man, Johanna. I'll send you a picture of my first born. My

138

wife is due next month. I'm also a loyal American. But. . . you. I still don't understand you."

"What's to understand, Mr. Hollinger?"

"Whose side are you on?"

"I told you before: on the side that wins, or in other words on the side of sound finance."

"Hah! You mean both sides then. Everyone knows the Germans still have a stash hidden in this country."

She spun around to leave. Glancing over her shoulder, she said, "A time is coming, in a few years, when there will be no sides."

"Yeah, yeah, I know. We'll all be one. Don't count on it."

Hollinger watched her walk across the lobby and disappear through the revolving doors to the street. She was talking as crazy as McCreedy.

Twenty

General George Patton took the call inside his country command post at three in the afternoon.

"General?" the frantic voice said over the telephone line.

"Yeah?"

"It's Matt."

Patton had a special place in his heart for General Manton Eddy, one of Patton's Third Army commanders whose soldiers were the first to cross the Rhine only a few weeks before, ahead of British General Montgomery. "Yeah, Matt? What is it?"

"General," Eddy blurted, out of breath, "you're not going to believe this. It's too damn near incredible."

"Slow down. What won't I believe? By the way, where the hell have you been all afternoon?"

"I'm at a salt mine near a village called Merkers."

Patton went to his map on the wall. Merkers was in Werra, in the Thuringia Mountains, a short driving distance away. "What the hell you doing there?"

"Checking out a couple stories. First, we found a cave with, hell, there must be a billion dollars in German money in it. A billion dollars!"

Patton had been briefed by a member of Eisenhower's staff in March that, according to rumours, the Nazis had hid their gold somewhere in southern Germany. Was this it? "Piss on the paper money. Did you find the damn gold?"

"No. At least not yet. But I think I know where it is. Or where it might be."

Patton was growing impatient. "What the hell you talking about?"

"Listen, General. There's a big steel door down there in the mine."

"Well, open it, Matt!"

"We can't."

"Why the hell not!"

"Sir, it's this way. We found two men of the local Reichsbank. They claim they don't have the keys. They say the only way to get in is blow the door open."

"So, blow it open. What the hell's the problem?"

"You say so."

"Anyway, what's the second story?"

"We found another cave. A few miles away."

"Well?" Patton shouted into the receiver.

"Sir, we found some of the strangest aircraft you ever did see. About half the size of regular fighter. And there's no room for a pilot. Somebody said they look radio-controlled. The place is deserted. No Jerries. Everybody must have flown the coop. You gotta see these things, general. Oh, by the way, there's also a bigger version of the funny aircraft. Just one. It was under some camouflage netting. Hell, this thing is something right out of Buck Rogers or. . . Superman. . . I don't know."

Patton sighed, and said, "I better call Ike."

BERN, SWITZERLAND—APRIL 6

Hollinger woke up from a deep sleep. "Hello," he grouched into the receiver, flicking the light on inside his third-floor hotel room.

"Wesley?"

"Yeah, who is this?"

"The Bern office. Did I catch you in bed?"

Hollinger recognized the fatherly voice of OSS Director Allen Dulles. "Well, sir," he said, sitting up, squinting at his wrist watch, "it *is* four in the morning."

Dulles chuckled. "Someone will be coming to your door. He has a grey suit, dark hair."

"But, sir—" Hollinger wanted to ask how soon he should expect the visitor, but heard nothing except for the dial tone. The OSS agent barely had time to throw a night robe over his pyjamas before he heard a soft knock. "Holy, hell!" He stumbled slowly to the door, rubbing his eyes.

Another knock.

"Hollinger."

"Yeah, yeah, keep your shirt on."

"Let me in."

Hollinger opened up. It was the man in the grey suit, dark hair, about thirty or so. "Yeah?"

The man brushed past, stopped, smiled, and said, "You want to meet General Patton?"

Hollinger shrugged. "Sure, why not. Who wouldn't?"

"Be ready in thirty minutes. I'll wait. Mr. Dulles wants me to escort you to the airfield."

"You mean I really am going to meet him?"

The man nodded. "Damn right. Come on, hurry up."

Hohenlychen, Germany

Colonel Geinns thought it pitiful how Heinrich Himmler had been reduced to working out of a cramped compartment aboard a train that Himmler called his Steirmark Headquarters.

Geinns entered the room stacked to the ceiling with files and saluted his boss. "Heil Hitler."

Himmler stood up. "Heil Hitler."

"You sent for me, Herr Reichsfuehrer."

"So, Herr Colonel, word tells me that the Luftwaffe tried to destroy the V-4 aircraft. Is that true, colonel?"

Geinns cleared his throat. "Yes, Herr Reichsfuehrer, that was a rumour. It doesn't matter. The Americans came down on us too soon. We all had to flee."

Himmler grunted and said, "That's the least of our problems right now. I want you to do something for me."

"Anything, Herr Reichsfuehrer."

"Where is your group of scientists?"

"A resort in the Harz Mountains, ordered there by the Fuehrer."

"You mean ordered by Bormann, do you not?"

"Sir?"

"Never mind. How close are the Americans?"

"Last report, twenty miles from the barracks. But the Americans are moving away from them. They've veered north for the moment."

"Do the barracks have phone service?"

"Yes, Herr Reichsfuehrer. A lot of static, however."

"I want you to run a wiretap on the phone lines, and I want you to search all letters."

"Of all the scientists, Herr Reichsfuehrer?"

"No, just one. Karl Zeller."

"Zeller?"

"Yes, Zeller. I want you to call me as soon as you find out he has made any contact with Herr Martin Bormann. Dismiss. Heil Hitler." Himmler turned and sat down, as Geinns left through a side door.

Himmler smirked to himself, making a notation in his diary. How lucky he was to find the information in a stashed away file, one of those that had been moved in a hurry from his last headquarters at Birken-hain with the Allies closing in. So, it seemed Zeller knew the Kiss-Ass's family. Was this a coincidence?

Twenty-one

Hitler listened to his elated Minister of Propaganda Dr. Josef Goebbels over the static of the telephone connection running into the Fuehrer-bunker.

"Mein Fuehrer, I congratulate you," Goebbels gasped. "The Jew American leader Franklin D. Rosenfeldt has just died. It was written in the stars by our astrologers that an important event would come in the second half of April. Don't you see, this is the turning point for Germany."

The Fuehrer could only nod and say, "That is good Goebbels. But it is too late."

"Don't say that, mein Fuehrer."

"But it *is* too late. I have been betrayed. By Himmler. By Goering. By the German people. They are not worthy of me."

"I have not betrayed you, mein Fuehrer. I shall be by your side. To the end."

HERSFELD, GERMANY

Generals Eisenhower, Eddy, and Patton discussed President Roosevelt's death as they made their way to the depths of a mine shaft aboard a creaky elevator.

"Shit, how old is this thing," Patton said with an uneasy grin, referring to the elevator, to change the subject. "I hope it doesn't come loose before it hits the bottom."

"Shut up, George," Allied Supreme Commander Dwight D. Eisenhower said, unimpressed.

"You know, if we all died here," Patton kidded, "there would be a few instant promotions in the Army."

Eisenhower grunted. "Quit it, George! That's not funny."

Then, with a mighty jerk, the elevator stopped. They were 1,500 feet below the surface. They walked into a huge hall measuring approximately seventy-five feet by a hundred and fifty feet. What they saw could have been right out of an epic Hollywood movie. Covering the floor were thousands of opened cotton bags containing gold coins and bars, all numbered on the outside. Loose paper money lined the left wall.

Eisenhower let out a whistle. "What's the tally? Has anybody counted the stuff?"

"We sure have," Eddy answered, pulling out a neatly folded piece of paper from his pocket. "At least we've started. Seven thousand bags of coins, weighing twenty-five pounds each. We still haven't counted all the valises along the far wall. But they hold gold and silver eyeglass frames, watches, wedding rings, gold and silver fillings, and such." Eddy lowered his voice. "These, I've heard, are from the concentration camps, sir."

"What else you got?" Eisenhower said, solemnly.

Eddy's eyes concentrated on his sheet. "All told, two hundred and fifty tons of gold. All the European paper currencies are here, sir. Almost three billion Reichsmarks. Ninety-eight million French francs. And there's the works of art, looted from the famous galleries of Europe. We estimate about 400 tons of artwork alone."

Eisenhower turned to Patton. "George, what are you going to do with all this?"

"Well, I've got that figured out, Ike." Patton rubbed his chin. "I'm going to melt down some of the gold so that every man in the Third Army would own a medallion of the European campaign. Most of it, I'd wait until those Congress bastards in Washington hold back our military funding. Then I'll just come down here and we'll have all the money we need for new weapons."

Eisenhower put his head down. "I never should have asked. Let's go, George. I want to talk to you."

Patton and Eisenhower returned to the elevator. As the machine began the ascent, Eisenhower said, "It's about those funny aircraft you showed me this morning."

"What about them, Ike?"

"You'll see. Wait until we get to the top."

The two didn't speak again until they reached the surface, and stepped off the elevator.

"George," Eisenhower said, "I want you to meet someone. Remember that young man in civilian clothes you saw before we went down the shaft?"

"Yeah. You mean that fellah over there?" Patton pointed across the rocky clearing. He wondered why the superbly dressed man wasn't in uniform.

"That's him." Eisenhower waved for the man to come over.

Wesley Hollinger was nervous. It seemed like an eternity before Eisenhower and Patton had popped to the surface. "Yes, sir," he croaked.

"George, meet Wesley Hollinger."

Patton shook hands with the agent. "Pleased to meet you, Mr. Hollinger."

Hollinger cleared his throat. He was surprised at how high Patton's voice was. "The pleasure is all mine, General Patton."

"So what's up?" Patton asked, his eyes darting from Eisenhower to the American civilian. "Who the hell are you, anyway?"

"General. . . sir. . . those strange aircraft you saw recently. . ."

"Yeah?"

"I have been asked—no. . . ordered—to tell you that you are not to divulge that you saw them or even heard about them. They do not exist."

"Why the hell not?"

"Because the whole thing is out of your hands. It is not a military matter."

"How the hell could that be? They're obviously military aircraft! What gives, Ike?"

"Shut up and listen to the man, George."

"General Patton," Hollinger continued, braver by the second, "I have a communiqué here from Washington handing over all authority—anything regarding these aircraft—to my department. We are also asking you to lift the Third Army guards from the area once we move in."

"Let me see the letter," Patton demanded, hand out, his eyes glaring at Hollinger.

"Of course, sir." Hollinger dug for the evidence in his suit jacket.

Patton read the paper quickly. "Son of a bitch! So, you're with the OSS. Why didn't you say so in the first place? Well, I'll be a—"

She read the dispatch delivered to her Secret Service desk with disinterest. It didn't say much, only that Wesley said he was still in good spirits and well fed. But still no word on when he was coming home.

Roberta rose from her chair to remove a file from her cabinet. It was near the end of the workday. It was then that it hit her. . . a crippling pain in her stomach that doubled her over. She dug her nails into the arm rests to pull herself back to her chair, catching her breath at the same time.

Was this it? A month early? And with Wesley so far away?

BERLIN—APRIL 14

Bormann laughed to himself when Goebbels arrived that day at the Fuehrerbunker. Dr. Goebbels kept his word with the Fuehrer. And it only took two days. He would stand by Hitler's side. To the end, if need be. What a fool Goebbels was. They were all fools.

"I will tell the Fuehrer you are here, Herr Goebbels," Bormann notified the limping Propaganda Minister, stopping him in the hall with a cold stare.

Goebbels bowed his head slightly, his wife and six children standing off to the side. "Thank you, Herr Bormann. But the Fuehrer knows I'm—"

"Stay here. The Fuehrer may be resting." Bormann turned into Hitler's office.

"Why do you let that grotesque man bully you?" Goebbels wife, Magda, whispered.

"Hush, my dear." Goebbels leaned on his cane.

Dr. Josef Goebbels was a forty-eight-year-old dwarf of a man. He hated Jews more than any other Nazi leader. As a result of osteomyelitis, an inflammation of the bone marrow as a child, his left leg was four inches shorter than his right. He was cursed with a permanent limp and little strength to his left side. When the Nazi movement began, he had sworn absolute loyalty to Hitler. And now he wished to be Hitler's most noble of knights. At work, Goebbels was the leading Nazi propagandist, the cultural dictator over domestic German life. At play, he was known to have many affairs with high-class German women.

Bormann returned quickly. "The Fuehrer is ready to receive you now, Herr Goebbels."

Roberta was sitting up, fully dressed, when Colonel Lampert arrived at the hospital early next morning.

"I came as soon as I could."

"Thank you."

"How are you?"

"False call," she sighed.

Lampert shook his head. "You must take better care of yourself, Roberta. You are working too hard. You only have a month to go. See here, I should tell you that I have made arrangements for someone else to do your paperwork for the next few months."

"But, sir." She pouted. "I'll go crazy. I've nothing to do."

"Now, now. Let's not have any of that. You're to stay home until your time comes. It's already been taken care of. No arguments."

"Yes, sir," she relented.

"Have you cabled Wesley?"

"No, I haven't, colonel."

"Why not?"

"I. . . don't want him to worry. He must have enough things on his mind at the moment, whatever they are."

"Yes, I suppose so." He moved towards her. "Here, my dear, let me help you to my auto. You don't look well."

"Thanks, colonel."

Twenty-two

Himmler held the cable from Geinns in his hands, inside his latest headquarters at Ziethen Castle on the Baltic Coast, east of Lubeck. It had taken Geinns most of that week to dig up the dirt on scientist Karl Zeller. One wiretapped telephone conversation between Zeller and Bormann was the proof. Himmler looked down and read.

B: They were not destroyed. Why?

Z: No time. Patton's army found them.

B: Intact?

Z: Yes.

B: The blueprints, are they safe?

Z: Yes.

B: Goodbye.

Z: Goodbye.

Although Heinrich Himmler was on the run from the Russians, he still loathed seeing anybody stabbing him in the back. Zeller and Bormann were in cahoots. They had sworn a pact. Were Bormann and Zeller trying to escape with V-4 blueprints and deal with the Americans? Himmler knew he couldn't get at Bormann because he was too close to the Fuehrer. So, he'd go after Zeller, instead.

Himmler opened his door.

His adjutant, Ludwig Hahn, had a telephone receiver to his ear. "Yes, Herr Reichsfuehrer?"

"Get me Colonel Geinns on the phone, immediately."

"Yes, Herr Reichsfuehrer." The adjutant spoke into the phone. "Yes, I will tell my superior. Thank you." He hung up.

"Tell me what?"

"Herr Reichsfuehrer! Our people have located Count Bernadotte of the Swedish Red Cross."

"They have?"

"Yes."

"Finally. Where's he been?"

"The Swedish Embassy in Lubeck."

"I will keep that in mind."

"Do you wish to speak to him in person?"

"Not now, you fool."

"Yes, Herr Reichsfuehrer. But you—"

"Sometime soon, perhaps."

HARZ MOUNTAINS

Zeller was bound, gagged, and whisked from his bunk inside the barracks in the cool of the evening by two SS guards and dragged outside into the darkness of the compound. Wearing only a long night-shirt, Zeller shivered. Two guards pushed the scientist to his knees.

Colonel Geinns walked up, his boots crunching the gravel. "For crimes against the state, Karl Zeller, you are to be shot on orders from Heinrich Himmler. Do you have any last words?"

Zeller nodded.

"Release the cloth from his mouth," Geinns demanded, and waited for one of the guards to obey.

"Yes, I have something to say," Zeller gasped, his breath steaming the air.

"What is it? Quickly."

"Save yourselves. United States officials have files on Nazi atrocities. They are receiving more and more such information all the time. They know about the torture and the Jewish concentration camps. Run while you can. You, Geinns are mentioned. You and Himmler. Run. Run."

"Shoot him!" Geinns yelled.

Two revolvers flashed in the night. Four bullets later, Zeller lay dead on the stones.

Lake Lucerne

Hollinger and McCreedy had drinks in their hands on the hotel terrace. "Shakes you up, don't it?" McCreedy said.

Hollinger agreed, nodding. "Yeah, that it does."

They looked over the lake and the Swiss mountains, glittering in the moonlight. They had come outside to get a breath of air after reading the printed reports, only a few days old. Belsen and Buchenwald concentration camps had been liberated by British and American troops. The full horror of Nazi crimes were now evident. At Belsen, near Hamburg, the British saw 10,000 unburied dead and over 40,000 starving, sick, and dying prisoners, exposed to the elements. The Americans found Buchenwald, near Weimar, in similar ghastly condition. Twenty thousand were still alive, barely. Thousands dead.

McCreedy guzzled his wine, the moonlight reflecting off his glasses. "I still have to wonder about something, the cynic that I am."

"What?"

"According to our sources, Himmler is responsible for. . . these. . ."

"Horrors?" Hollinger said.

"Yeah, horrors. For some reason Bormann is trying awfully hard to convince us that Himmler is the man that the Allies will hold responsible for the concentration camps."

"So?"

"So, pal, Bormann is Hitler's confidant. Bormann had to have some say in it. The orders to eliminate the Jews would have come through Hitler's office."

"Didn't I suspect Bormann from the beginning?"

"Yes, you did, I admit."

Hollinger set his glass down on the outdoor table. "Messy damn business."

"You know what I think, Wesley, old boy?" McCreedy turned his back to Hollinger.

"What do you think, Tom?"

"Our side wants Bormann's neck, along with all the fancy machinery. The OSS brass, I think, are laying a trap for him."

"Why do you figure that?"

"He knows too much. He has the goods on Dulles, on Nazi bank accounts, you name it. He can't be trusted. Once the public gets all the facts about the camps, Bormann will be a marked man. And you know what else? Bormann knows it."

"You think so?"

"I'm sure he does. He's no dummy. Our deal with him is not going to be as cut and dried as we think. There has to be some reason why he's held up in Berlin, waiting for the Russians. He's up to something."

"You think he may try his own escape?"

"It's highly possible," McCreedy said. "In fact, I'd bet on it."

"You may be right. But we still have our OSS orders. All we can do is wait until he makes his move."

Twenty-three

Martin Bormann stood back from the others and viewed the dismal morning scene in the crowded Chancellery garden. Today was a public holiday for Adolf Hitler's fifty-sixth birthday.

Everyone did their best to ignore the crunch of Russian artillery fire off in the distance. General Zhuvov's victorious troops had now reached the north-eastern suburbs of the once great German capital. And here was the Fuehrer, looking every bit of twenty years older, accompanied by Hermann Goering, Heinrich Himmler and Josef Goebbels, pinning medals on eager members of the Hitler Youth, and shaking hands with them. Also in the throng of bodies stood Albert Speer and Joachim von Ribbentrop, both hollow eyed. Bormann grunted to himself. What a picture they were. And what about the Hitler Youth? They were chosen to be the rear line of the nation's defense for the pathetic Nazi leadership. They would fight the Russians to the last. That wouldn't take too long. Hours? Minutes?

Bormann was disgusted. So deplorable. So distressing. More needless deaths. He looked across the garden and caught Goering's eye, and they shook their heads at each other.

Goering emerged from the depths of the bunker shortly after noon to find Bormann smoking, waiting opposite a battered concrete wall, while the others were below celebrating what was sure to be Hitler's last birthday on earth. The Luftwaffe leader lumbered over to the Little Fat Man. They stood two feet apart, Goering in his new, clean khaki

155

uniform, tailored to his body, and Bormann in his equally-startling white Reichsleiter tunic, riding breeches and glossy riding boots.

"Blood brother, Herr Bormann."

"Blood brother, Herr Goering."

"It just came through. Nuremberg has fallen to the Americans," Goering said, gravely.

Bormann huffed. "The site of our Party rallies. Does the Fuehrer know?"

"Yes. That's not all. Marshall Rokossovski's Second White Russian Front has moved along the Lower Odor and has taken Pomerania and Mecklenburg. And all the Fuehrer can say is, 'and now it's a fight for Berlin. The Russians will suffer their greatest defeat.' He almost looked relieved. When I left, the Fuehrer was speaking with Admiral Doenitz behind closed doors."

Bormann puffed on his cigarette. "Yes, Goering, and do you know why?"

"I'm sure I can guess. Herr Doenitz will be the new Fuehrer."

"Yes, and in particular Hitler is advising the admiral to establish his headquarters at Obersalzberg, before the Russians encircle Berlin and cut us off."

"Then despite what Hitler said about the upcoming Russian defeat, he must admit that the end is near."

"Yes, but we—*you*—can do something before Doenitz takes over."

"What can I do?"

"You can seize power yourself, before the Fuehrer dies."

"How? And why take that chance at this point in time if we are waiting to deal with the OSS?"

"Because you can deal better as the new Fuehrer. Listen to me, you fool. Did the Fuehrer not make you—by decree—his official successor on June 29, 1941?"

"Yes, but—"

"Here's what you can do. Where were you planning to go after Berlin?"

"I will return to my mountain chalet at Berchtesgaden, of course."

With your family and art treasures, you fat cow, Bormann thought. "Of course. At your chalet, you are only a few miles from the Swiss border. Perfect. I want you to know that Doenitz will not be accepted as the new leader. The land forces know that you were confirmed as Hitler's successor. They will listen only to you, not a navy man."

Goering felt proud. "They will?"

"Yes, they will. I am certain of it. I would stake my life on it. Besides, you must be the new leader so that you can take care of Himmler and give him his just desserts."

"Himmler? Why Himmler? What does he have to do with this? Is he planning to take power?"

Bormann inhaled slowly, and blew out some smoke. "Because he has our scientists held up, under SS guard, in the Harz Mountains. And he killed one of them."

"He did! Who?"

"My contact, Zeller."

Goering's face reddened. "The butcher!"

"Yes, blood brother. Himmler is and always was a butcher. If we don't get rid of him, he'll cut his own negotiations with the Americans, and use the scientists to do it. What we have to do is deliver the scientists and the—"

"The blueprints," Goering interrupted. "Are they out of harm's way?"

Bormann smiled for a moment, stamping his cigarette into the ground. With Zeller dead, Bormann's situation appeared grave in one respect. His smile faded as he thought of his line to the OSS, now cut. "Very safe. And Himmler doesn't know a thing about them."

"Wait. What is that?" Goering looked to the sky. Miles away. Dark specks. . . and streams of white. High-altitude aircraft.

"American bombers," Bormann said the words for the Luftwaffe leader.

"And it's only fitting on Hitler's birthday," Goering added.

"Yes, isn't it. We had better get below before the fireworks start. But first, do you agree to take power."

"When?"

"When I tell you. Go to your chalet and sit tight."

"I can see one problem."

"What problem?"

"The Fuehrer. What if he objects?"

"Don't you worry about the Fuehrer." Bormann smiled. "I'll look after that. All you have to do is to notify the Fuehrer of your intentions and I will see to the rest. I guarantee it. Besides, he seems more relaxed now that Eva has been here a few days."

Hitler's mistress of twelve years, pretty Eva Braun, had arrived to join her lover on the fifteenth of April. The German public knew very little about her and her association with the Fuehrer. Word in the bunker was that the two would be married shortly.

"Ah, Eva," Goering uttered, sadly. "It is too bad she has come for her wedding. . . and her funeral."

Bormann nodded in agreement. "Yes, she never was very bright."

WUSTROW

Two things were certain to Heinrich Himmler upon his return to his headquarters by aircraft later on that day: he would never visit Berlin again by choice, and he would never see Hitler alive again. The Fuehrer was lost in his own world of drugs and phantom armies made up of young boys ready to die for a cause not worth anything any more. Before he left Berlin, Himmler had already put his plans into place. He conferred with his Gestapo man in the city, Heinrich Muller, giving instructions to murder all the important political prisoners involved in the July 20, 1944 bomb plot to assassinate Hitler.

Himmler entered his office. Now, in light of recent news, he had to make more plans. According to SS reports, Patton's men had found the radio-controlled V-4's. Had the Americans got word of the slave labour there? Himmler knew he had no collateral to negotiate with the Allies, except for the scientists.

He called his tired adjutant in.

"Yes, Herr Reichsfuehrer?" Hahn answered.

"We can't turn in, not yet. I want extra SS guards on the scientists at Bleicherode. They are to be taken further south, near the Swiss border." Himmler had a map spread out on his desk. "Bavaria. There's some old army barracks at Oberammergau."

"Are these orders from Berlin?"

"No. They are my orders. Do it. I will accept all responsibility."

"Yes, Herr Reichsfuehrer."

"Then, send a memo to all concentration camp commandants telling them to release all remaining camp prisoners."

"All of them, Herr Reichsfuehrer?"

"Yes. Jews. Men, women, children. Everybody. Also, in the memo I want it stated that all crematoriums were used to kill the victims of war epidemics. Do I make myself clear?"

"Yes, Herr Reichsfuehrer."

"Another thing, get me Count Bernadotte of the Swedish Red Cross. Right away!"

"At this hour?"

"Yes, at this hour! Step to it!"

"Yes, Herr Reichsfuehrer."

"Get back to me."

Twenty-four

The day did not start out favourably for those seven hundred who still remained out of blind loyalty in the Fuehrerbunker. News had arrived, threefold: Nine hundred four-engined Royal Air Force bombers had turned Bremen to ashes. The First French Army had taken Stuttgart. The Second British Army were pounding at the doors of Hamburg. Still, Adolf Hitler held hope that Berlin would not go the way of Stuttgart and Nuremberg before it.

His reason?

SS General Felix Steiner was given command of the 11th Panzer Army, ordered by the Fuehrer to head southeast to slice the Soviet Red Army in half and lift the siege on Berlin. Rising at nine that morning, Hitler was expecting a positive report from Steiner. Soon. Hitler had great confidence in Steiner, who had stopped the Red Army advance only weeks before at Pomerania. Could he do it again? In Hitler's world, Steiner could. Never mind that the general had only a few thousand men with only a handful of usable tanks.

Tagebuch in hand, Bormann saw the act unfold; a pitiful scene it was too. In a conference, the overly-optimistic Army Chief of Staff General Hans Krebs was giving Hitler the verbal report of Steiner's progress. According to Krebs, the battle was actually going quite nicely for Steiner. Bormann knew better. What a liar Krebs was. Bormann's suspicions were confirmed when General Alfred Jodl interrupted the meeting by telling Hitler that the city was surrounded. A grin formed on Bormann's lips, then faded quickly. He sat up, waiting for the truth to clear the air.

"Where is Steiner? What's he doing?" Hitler asked Jodl.

"He is not doing. . . that well," Jodl admitted. "The Russians have broken through."

The Fuehrer went into a rage, shaking, stomping his feet. "Everyone has deserted me! Cowards! That's what they are! All cowards!" Then he sank into his chair, holding his throat, breathing heavy. His body began to twitch. He lowered his voice, and uttered, "The war is lost. Lost. There is nothing left to fight for."

Bormann gulped. Here was the man who he had admired for so many years. Now look at him. "If you lose faith, mein Fuehrer, then everything is lost. Is it not?"

Hitler nodded, his head jerking. "Yes."

"There is still a way out, mein Fuehrer."

Hitler stared at the wall. "How, Bormann? Tell me, how."

"Leave for your Berchtesgaden estate at once. From there, a neutral country can take you in. Spain or Argentina, perhaps. With the rugged terrain in the mountains, we can fend off the Allies for weeks or months while someone negotiates on your behalf."

Hitler shook his head. It took him a long time to answer. "Himmler told me the same thing yesterday by telephone. But there is no safe haven for me. For the rest of you, that's another story." He looked up at Bormann, his eyes glassy. "Bormann?"

Bormann stood, clicked his heels. "Yes, mein Fuehrer."

"I will never leave Berlin. Do you hear me? I want you to destroy all documents in the Fuehrerbunker."

"Yes, mein Fuehrer. I will see to it right away." Perfect, thought Bormann, showing no emotion.

Berlin—April 23

In the afternoon, Bormann peeled the telegram off the machine in the communications room. Else Krueger gazed from afar. As she turned away, he grinned to himself, heading for Hitler's office.

"Mein, Fuehrer, I think you should read this," he said, at the open door.

Hitler was staring off, his mind absent of thought. Patting his dog, Blondi, he glanced up from his desk. "What is it, Bormann?" Hitler took the telegram and read it.

MY FUEHRER! IN VIEW OF YOUR DECISION TO REMAIN AT
YOUR POST IN THE FORTRESS OF BERLIN, DO YOU AGREE
THAT I TAKE OVER, AT ONCE, THE TOTAL LEADERSHIP OF
THE REICH WITH FULL FREEDOM OF ACTION, AT HOME AND
ABROAD, AS YOUR DEPUTY IN ACCORDANCE WITH YOUR
DECREE OF 29 JUNE 1941? IF NO REPLY IS RECEIVED BY TEN
O'CLOCK TONIGHT, I SHALL TAKE IT FOR GRANTED THAT
YOU HAVE LOST YOUR FREEDOM OF ACTION AND SHALL
CONSIDER THE CONDITIONS OF YOUR DECREE AS FULFILLED,
AND SHALL ACT FOR THE BEST INTEREST OF OUR COUNTRY
AND OUR PEOPLE. YOU KNOW WHAT I FEEL FOR YOU IN THIS
GRAVEST HOUR OF MY LIFE. WORDS FAIL ME TO EXPRESS
MYSELF. MAY GOD PROTECT YOU, AND SPEED YOU QUICKLY
HERE IN SPITE OF IT ALL.

YOUR LOYAL,

HERMANN GOERING

Glassy-eyed, Hitler said, slowly, "It doesn't matter who arranges the capitulation, now. Goering could do it, I suppose, although he's corrupt and a drug addict."

Bormann did not expect this. He stepped forward, knowing that he would have to act quickly. "But mein Fuehrer, the Reichmarshall *demands* an answer from you by ten tonight. That. . . that is high treason."

Hitler's mood quickly changed. He squeezed the paper in his fist. A slow burn began to heat inside him. "You're right. The traitor! An ultimatum! Giving me until ten o'clock tonight! How dare he!"

"Yes, he is a traitor. What should we do, mein Fuehrer?"

Hitler pounded his desk with the flat side of his palm, then calmed himself in order to speak. "Arrest him, that's what! Send a telegram to him at once, informing him that his actions are high treason to the Party and its leader and that the penalty should be death."

Bormann's eyebrows raised a notch. "Death, mein Fuehrer?"

Hitler waved his hand. "But due to his earlier services to the Party, that will not be the case. He must resign at once. Tell him that all I require from him is a yes or no. Send it."

Bormann wrote out the telegram as his leader required and sent it off, signing Hitler's name to it. Then, thinking about it more, he sent off a second message, also under the Fuehrer's name.

> DECREE OF 6.29.41 IS RESCINDED BY MY SPECIAL INSTRUC-
> TION. MY FREEDOM OF ACTION UNDISPUTED. I FORBID ANY
> MOVE BY YOU IN THE DIRECTION INDICATED BY YOU.

LUBECK, GERMANY

They heard the rumble overhead nearly an hour before midnight and ran to the cellar below the Swedish Embassy. Electricity cut off, on candlelight only, Count von Bernadotte of the Swedish Red Cross and Heinrich Himmler waited out the bomber raid. They did not emerge until midnight. Still by candlelight, they continued their negotiations in the Count's study, their fifth meeting since the early part of the year.

Himmler was exhausted and on the verge of a nervous breakdown. "Hitler is determined to die in his bunker," he said to von Bernadotte. "Therefore I came to cut my own peace terms as I see fit."

"Go on."

"Due to your excellent connections, I need you to send a message through your government to Eisenhower. In order to stop unnecessary further bloodshed, you can tell him that I—the military power in northern Germany, Norway, Scandinavia, Holland, and military leader of the Army Group Vistula—will hereby surrender my forces to Eisenhower on the western front to allow the Anglo-American forces to march east, before the Russians move in. Furthermore, I have in custody a team of scientists that are sure to be of use to the Americans in the future."

"Where are they?"

"Confined to a set of army barracks near Oberammergau, in the Bavarian Alps, only a few miles from the Austrian border."

"Is that so? Well, then, I want you to do something for me."

"What is it?" Himmler asked.

"All Scandinavian prisoners must be set free, immediately. Before I even contact my government."

"Immediately?"

"Yes," von Bernadotte insisted.

"Agreed. I will also be willing to talk with the Swedish section of the

World Jewish Congress to *liberate* all those Jews under SS control. I will let bygones be bygones."

Von Bernadotte stared at the man in black. "That is very big of you, I'm sure, seeing that it was you who imprisoned them."

Himmler shook his finger. "I was only following orders."

"As you say."

"It's true. I was following orders. Written orders. Do you know who from?"

"Who?"

"Hitler's secretary, Martin Bormann. He's the one responsible for millions of deaths. He and the Fuehrer put it all together to eliminate a race, to do away with undesirables. And I can prove it. I have the documentation. You can tell that to the Americans and the World Jewish Congress. In fact, please do."

"Perhaps, I will."

"Good." Himmler stood. "I must go."

They shook hands and Himmler left in his armour-plated Mercedes.

BERLIN—APRIL 24

Into the early morning hours, Bormann was beside himself. Now Hitler wanted to draft another telegram to Goering to say that the Luftwaffe leader was too feeble to act on Germany's behalf, with no further mention of treason or death penalty. Bormann wheeled into the communications room and sent off his own message to the SS commandant at Obersalzberg, near Goering's mountain chalet. The commandant's orders were to arrest Goering and shoot him.

Finished, Bormann sat back. Should the time come, he'd have to explain how Goering had died.

BERCHTESGADEN

At daybreak, Standartenfuehrer Frank of the SS entered Goering's chalet and said, "Herr Reichmarshall, you are under arrest on orders from Berlin. High treason."

He then pushed a single bullet into a pistol, set it on the night table, and left the Luftwaffe leader standing there at the entrance in his night robe.

It was obvious to Goering that one option was to take his own life.

Watching the SS officer stepping into his auto, the Reichmarshall realized without a doubt that Bormann had stabbed him in the back.

The little boot-licking kiss-ass hadn't changed. A Bormann guarantee meant nothing.

BERCHTESGADEN—APRIL 25

When the commandant returned the next morning with a detachment of SS guards, he was amazed to find Goering very much alive and waiting for him upstairs in full uniform.

"Well," Goering said, "what did you expect?"

Flicking his wrist, Frank turned to his guards, who began to raise their guns.

Then the air-raid siren blared. Explosions rocked the chalet, sending everyone to the floor. Wall plaster crashed down. During a brief pause, one guard groped for a window. The sound of engines came upon them quickly. "American bombers! Here come some more!"

"Run for the basement!" Goering yelled, over the roar. "This way!"

The raid was over in minutes. Goering and the SS men emerged from the cellar. Stunned, they looked at each other and the surroundings. The chalet was completely destroyed.

BERLIN

Bormann received the telegram from Frank. So Goering had escaped a bombing raid and was presently in the SS's custody, was he. At least he was out of the way. Bormann crumpled the paper and threw it in his office trashcan. He would order Frank to keep him there, and guard him. Bormann was suddenly reminded of the day the news had broke of Rudolf Hess's departure.

Hess's adjutant, Karlheinz Pintsch, had arrived at Hitler's Berghof hideaway in the mountains with the information that Hess had upped and flown to Scotland to talk peace with the British. The first person Hitler had screamed for was Martin Bormann, then Hess's Chief of Staff. He had rushed into Hitler's room. The Fuehrer ordered Bormann to reach Goering, Ribbentrop, Himmler, and Goebbels by the fastest means possible, and to confine all guests to the upper floor. Bormann obeyed. Minutes later, with great pride, his parting words to Pintsch before the SS whisked him away were, "Captain Karlheinz Pintsch, you are under arrest. You will be held at Obersalzberg until a court of inquiry can be held into your part in the events of today. Heil Hitler." With Hess gone, it was the beginning of Bormann's rise to power as Hitler's confidant.

Now, four years later, high-ranking Goering was out of the picture.

Himmler was on the run. The SS men guarding the scientists would surely desert Himmler because they had sworn an oath to Hitler.

Goebbels would stay in Berlin to the end. The idiot.

Next. . . Hitler.

Bormann thought of his wife, Gerda, and their children. They too were at Berchtesgaden, not far away from Goering's estate. Bormann shut the door inside his office and telephoned an SS officer he knew at Berchtesgaden.

"Wilhelm, it is I, Bormann, at the Fuehrerbunker."

"Yes, Herr Reichsleiter."

Bormann took a deep breath. "I need to know, did my house make it through the bombing raid?"

"No, Herr Reichsleiter. It did not. But your family is all safe."

"Good. Listen to me closely. Get them out of there."

"How? What should I do?"

"Send them to the Austrian border in a Red Cross bus."

"I understand. That could work, yes. What is your situation there in Berlin, Herr Reichsleiter?"

"In peril. The city is surrounded by the Russians."

"And the Fuehrer? How is he?"

Bormann took another deep breath. "Alive. Just barely, that is. Living on drugs and chocolates."

Twenty-five

Allen Dulles rose from his padded chair and plunked himself on the edge of his desk to square away with Tom McCreedy and Wesley Hollinger.

"Gentlemen," the OSS Director began. "I called you here to tell you that some news may break in the next couple days concerning separate peace negotiations between the Germans and General Eisenhower. Gestapo leader Heinrich Himmler has been in touch with the Swedes, who are his intermediaries, claiming that he will, and I quote,"—Dulles eyed a sheet of paper in his hands—"*in order to stop unnecessary further bloodshed I will surrender my entire military forces of northern Germany, Norway, Scandinavia, Holland, as well as Army Group Vistula to General Dwight D. Eisenhower.* Unquote. He has also consented to free all the Jews under SS control."

McCreedy and Hollinger shot glances at each other.

"What you won't hear in the news," Dulles continued, "is that a unit of SS guards has Wernher von Braun and his team of scientists in custody at a German army camp not far from here in Bavaria, a place called Oberammergau. Whether they—the scientists, that is—have the blueprints for their weapons is not certain."

"So the team is Himmler's insurance, his ticket out?" Hollinger asked.

"You guessed it," Dulles replied. "At least he thinks it's his ticket out."

"I see. So, when do we move in?"

"When Patton takes the area. It's only a matter of time, Mr. Hollinger."

Hollinger had heard plenty of that before. He was bored in

169

Switzerland. He'd rather be back in England with his pregnant wife. Nothing was happening here. Only talk. "How much time?"

"Days. Berlin will fall shortly. The Russians are within artillery range of the Chancellery, where Hitler and some of his faithful are holding in their fortified bunker. When Berlin goes, so goes Germany. Germany capitulates, then you two, representing the OSS, are going to find the scientists."

"Bormann—how goes it with him?" McCreedy wanted to know.

"No word. As far as we know, Bormann's still alive, according to our OSS shortwave people in Germany. So's Hitler. So's Goebbels. So is Goering. Another thing about Bormann: Himmler claims that it was Bormann behind the Jewish concentration camp murders, and that he—Himmler—has the written proof, orders handed down from Hitler's office, signed by none other than our pal, Martin Bormann."

Hollinger grunted. "Does this mean we won't be cutting a deal with Bormann?"

"Right again," Dulles answered, without expression. "If this news gets out, it will change things dramatically. Hopefully, we can obtain the blueprints on our own, without Bormann, who our office now considers a war criminal, and who will be tried as such, providing we can get him before the Russians do."

"You don't suppose Bormann suspects Himmler's motives do you?"

Dulles thought about that. "If he doesn't at this time, he will when the news breaks of Himmler's plans to free the Jews."

"You seem certain that the news will break, sir," Hollinger concluded.

Dulles nodded. "It's a way of flushing Bormann out. Divide and conquer. Hitler's been using it for years. This time it's our turn."

McCreedy pursed his lips. "Then, sir, I presume that you don't expect Bormann to show up at our rendezvous point to take him to Switzerland?"

"No, I do not. I think he knows we're after him. Otherwise, we would have gotten out of Berlin by now. Last I heard, the city's surrounded."

Later, walking in the hall, McCreedy leaned into Hollinger. "We had Bormann pegged right, didn't we. He was trying awfully hard to convince us that Himmler was responsible for the concentration camps. Do we know what's going on, or not?"

They turned a corner and took a flight of stairs down. "Yeah," Hollinger admitted. "We know what's going on. Ah, hell, they're probably both to blame, anyway."

"I don't doubt it. I'll drink to that."

"I bet you will. But these are working hours, Tom." Hollinger felt for his wristwatch. "It's not even ten o'clock. We just had breakfast."

McCreedy smiled. "Well, buddy boy, I guess we're on alert. So Dulles says."

"Yeah, let's get this thing over with. I can't take any more sitting around."

McCreedy stopped Hollinger at the bottom of the stairs. "And you, Wesley, were right about something."

"And that was?"

"This is a messy business."

Hollinger smirked. "Wrong. I said it was a *damn* messy business."

"All right, I stand corrected."

BERLIN

The once-majestic Reich Chancellery, above the Fuehrerbunker, was now being shelled at random. Bormann could hear the massive masonry walls crashing down in the garden, where he and Goering had held their many private and treasonous walks. Then, one shell landed directly above, and shook the walls of Bormann's office. He looked up. All day long sulphur smoke and lime dust had been filling his nostrils as the bunker's ventilators sucked the destruction inside. The warm air was fast becoming unbearable. People were perspiring. They were grouchy, and they were complaining of headaches and shortness of breath.

But nothing could be done, except to tell the Russians to stop the shelling. . . or the bunker could surrender. Neither seemed likely, at least not for a while.

In the evening Bormann heard footsteps in the hall. Bormann turned the corner outside his office to find the slight of frame crack woman pilot, Hanna Reitsch, in flight gear, her leather helmet in her hand, her hair a tangled mess. Reitsch was held in awe by those in the Luftwaffe. Fearless, she had been known to successfully test some of the fastest aircraft in the world, including the tricky and dangerous Me-163 rocket fighter. "Fraulein Reitsch! What are you doing here?"

"I must see the Fuehrer at once, Herr Reichsleiter."

Bormann stood there a long time. He could see that she was determined about something. "Of course." He turned away from her, then quickly turned back to ask, "How did you get through? The city is surrounded. The Russians are only blocks away, are they not?"

"I flew in, Herr Reichsleiter." She smiled.

Bormann shook his head. What lunacy this was in this underground madhouse. Everybody else was deserting Berlin and she was flying *in*. "Very well, come with me."

A minute later, Reitsch was pleading with Hitler face to face in his concrete study, while Eva Braun sat on a sofa across the room, sipping tea. "Mein Fuehrer, you must leave while there is still time. Why do you stay? Why do you deprive Germany of your life? You must live for your country that needs you. The people demand it. I, mein Fuehrer, can fly you out to safety."

Hitler sighed. "I don't doubt that you have the ability to do so. You are an outstanding pilot. But, no Hanna. If I die it is for the honour of our country. It is because as a soldier I must obey my own command that I would defend Berlin to the last. For you see, my dear girl, I believe that Berlin may be saved."

"But how?" Reitsch asked, startled, glancing back at Bormann in the doorway.

"General Wenck is moving his troops from the south. He will drive the Russians out. You will see." Just then, a shell burst above, shaking the bunker, causing ceiling dust to fall to the floor. Hitler handed the pilot a vial of poison from his baggy, dusty suit jacket. "Here, Hanna, take this, just in case you do not make it safely out of Berlin. We have reports of thousands of rapes in the streets." Reitsch took the vial in her small hand and stared at it. "Mein Fuehrer—"

"No," Hitler snapped, cutting her off before she could plead more. "My mind is made up."

Berlin—April 28

Bormann could not believe the news at first. But, then again, why should it have surprised him? He looked down at the dispatch that had been hurried over by a lowly courier from the Propaganda Ministry across the street from the Chancellery. It was just too incredible. The Ministry

172

picked up a BBC broadcast stating that Heinrich Himmler had been cutting surrender plans with Eisenhower through secret negotiations with the Swedes and Count von Bernadotte. And, it seemed, the Americans weren't considering any terms except for Unconditional Surrender.

"Thank you," Bormann said.

The courier fled to the corridor and the dangers of the outside.

Bormann turned the communications centre shortwave to Radio Stockholm, stalling for time before he would tell the Fuehrer. He listened intently. In minutes, he got the story. So, it was true. Bormann had mixed emotions. Himmler would soon be out of the way. Another one to add to the list. Hess. Goering. Now Himmler. Bormann gritted his teeth. He still had to relay the news to his leader.

When Hitler was informed, he went into a rage that Bormann had never seen, and he thought he had seen the worst when Goering tried to seize power. It was a hard deathblow for Hitler. He screamed, stomped his feet, and turned so red in the face that Bormann thought Hitler would explode. Once he recovered, he shouted at the small crowd made up of Eva Braun, Josef Goebbels, and Martin Bormann. At least, Hitler raged, Goering had asked the Fuehrer to relinquish command. Himmler, Hitler's most loyal of cohorts, had not even bothered to ask permission to act. He went and made plans on his own, the epitome of treachery for sure.

As he stood there in Hitler's room, Bormann thought back. Suspicious of Himmler for the last couple of days, Bormann saw how it all made sense to him. Himmler's liaison officer and SS representative at court, General Hermann Fegelein, brother-in-law to Eva Braun, had quietly deserted his post at the Fuehrerbunker on April 26. No one had noticed the disappearance until the next day, when a subordinate had gone looking for him. Hitler ordered an SS search party to find Fegelein, and find him they did, at home in civilian clothes in a district soon to be overrun by the Russians. Brought back to the bunker, Fegelein was stripped of his SS rank by Hitler and placed under heavy guard. In Bormann's mind and now Hitler's too, Fegelein had caught wind of the sinking SS ship.

Now Uncle Heiny's motives were definite enough. He craved total power.

Then Bormann thought of something else. The incriminating Berlin orders. *The extermination papers!* Would Himmler have. . .? No. . . he wouldn't. Wait. . . he. . . Bormann's knees began to buckle. No, Himmler would, if it meant saving his own ass. Why hadn't Bormann thought of it before? He knew his dealings with the OSS were in question once Zeller was shot. Bormann had the trumped-up paperwork, accusing Himmler, and only Himmler, of millions of deaths. But Himmler had the real thing. The Berlin orders. Bormann cursed. The deal for high tech blueprints—the Foo Fighter—for his safety was in jeopardy. What he had on Dulles and the American big businessmen would be nothing compared to what Uncle Heiny had on him, providing Himmler had filed the paperwork, which he probably had.

Himmler filed everything.

From the steps of the Chancellery, Bormann watched Reitsch take off in her single-engine airplane. He winced when the undercarriage barely cleared the Brandenburg Gate. Several shots rang out, obviously from Russian snipers. The aircraft banked away, unscathed. He breathed a sigh. Bormann liked Reitsch, but what a blind fool she was to risk her life now. This was Bormann's first time outside in days. From this vantage point he was shocked to see the city in ragged ruins. Although word had come through that Wenck had lost, for some strange reason the Russian shelling had ceased for the time being.

Reitsch's new orders were clear. She was to fly Ritter von Greim—the new Commander in Chief of the Luftwaffe, appointed by Hitler over Goering—to Plon, where the two would confer with Admiral Doenitz, and inform him that he was to arrest Heinrich Himmler on sight. "A traitor must never succeed me as Fuehrer!" Hitler had told Reitsch, minutes before, Bormann standing off to the side. "You must get out to insure that he will not."

Bormann quickly returned to the bunker below. He stopped at the guardhouse, and witnessed the next stage of Hitler's revenge against Himmler, involving General Hermann Fegelein. Led out to the Chancellery garden, the general was accused of having been an accomplice with Himmler. Then Fegelein was shot. Being Eva's brother-in-law had no bearing on whether he would live or die. Bormann turned away and descended again to the rancid Fuehrerbunker air.

She started to sign her name "Eva Braun." Then she realized her mistake, giggled lightly, and stroked out the "B" and wrote "Eva Hitler, born Braun." Bormann looked down at Hitler's wedding document, declaring that Hitler and Eva were of pure Aryan descent and free from hereditary disease. Stone-faced, Bormann signed as a witness inside the small conference room. An hour after midnight, the Fuehrer and Eva were now officially married, the conclusion of a decade-long affair. Too bad they only had hours or days at most to spend together as a new couple, Bormann thought. And too bad they couldn't go anywhere on their honeymoon.

Hitler thanked the man who married them, Walter Wagner, a municipal councillor who was fighting the Russians a few blocks away. Then the party began in Hitler's private apartment, complete with champagne. Hitler even invited the cooks. Bormann sipped from his glass and watched the smiling Hitler tell the others of the better days with party comrades true to the cause. Everyone seemed in good spirits, until more than an hour into Hitler's dialogue.

"Now it has ended," the Fuehrer said, his lips frowning. "And so has National Socialism. It will be a release for me to die, since I have been betrayed by old friends and businessmen abroad who once supported me."

Head down, Hitler walked away. This was Bormann's signal to follow Hitler. Bormann glanced around the room before he left. Everyone was crying. Goebbels, the secretaries, the cooks. Everyone... except Bormann.

By 4am, Hitler had drafted his Last Will. Bormann made the changes, and read it back to his dreary, tired leader one last time. *"As executor of this will, I appoint my most faithful Party comrade, Martin Bormann. He is given full legal authority to make all decisions. He is permitted to take out for my brothers and sisters whatever has any value as a personal memento or is necessary to maintain a modest standard of living."*

"Sign it, Bormann."

"I will be honoured to, mein Fuehrer. Thank you for your faith in—"

"Yes, yes. Now, read me the Political Testament."

"Certainly, mein Fuehrer."

Bormann flipped a page in his file and began. *"A number of men*

such as Martin Bormann, Dr. Goebbels, and others, including their
wives, have voluntarily joined me. They do not wish to leave the capital
of the Reich under any circumstances; they are willing to die with me.
Nevertheless, I must ask them to obey my request, and in this case to put
the interests of the nation above their own feelings. By their work and
loyalty as associates they will be just as close to me as I hope my spirit
will be to them; may it linger among them and accompany them always.
Let them be hard but never unjust; above all let them never allow fear to
influence their actions, and let them put the honour of the nation above
all else on earth. Finally, let them be conscious of the fact that our task
for the coming centuries is the continuing construction of the National
Socialist state, and this places every single person under an obligation
always to serve the common interest and to subordinate his own advan-
tages to this end."

Finished, Bormann glanced over the sheet. He snickered. Hitler had
fallen asleep in his chair.

Twenty-six

It had been raining for two days in the capital. By afternoon, the mood in the Fuehrerbunker was as dreary as the wet streets and overcast skies on the surface. And to add to the misery, General Zhukov's Red Army was only a block away from the Fuehrerbunker, and closing, yard by yard. No doubt the enemy would reach the Chancellery within a few hours. Forty-eight hours at most.

When the news of the situation reached the Fuehrer, he summoned to his apartment his faithful confidant since Hess's departure in 1941. The two were alone, door closed. Stooped over, Hitler appeared in a daze, an abrupt contrast to Bormann, who was bright, alert, and well dressed in his Reichsleiter uniform

"Bormann, I want you to wire Hanna for me."

"May I ask why, mein Fuehrer?"

"I want to live, Bormann."

Bormann stared, wide-eyed, at his leader. Why did the Fuehrer want to change his mind now? Who had put him up to this? Eva, probably, that hair-brained dimwit. And this now, after Hitler had given his tearful goodbyes to his bunker subordinates only hours before. Those present were all expecting their Third Reich leader to take his own life by nightfall.

"What does Fraulein Reitsch have to do with you living, mein Fuehrer?" Bormann finally asked.

"Because I want her to fly us out. Eva and I."

Bormann cleared his throat. "But, mein Fuehrer, even if I could

177

locate her on such short notice, which I doubt, how would she fly in and out with the Russians so close? The situation has changed. Rubble is covering the streets. She'd need a street as long as a runway for any single-engine aircraft to land or take off. She'd never make it."

"She can do it!" Hitler was shouting now, his face flushed. "She can do anything!"

Bormann stood his ground. "But will she want to do it, now?" he said, surprised that he had mustered up the courage to speak so boldly.

Fire in his eyes, Hitler screamed, "She will do anything I tell her to do. Go, go find her! Now!"

Bormann swallowed hard, bowed, and clicked his heels. "Yes, mein Fuehrer."

Hitler turned away, hands behind his back. End of discussion.

No one was going to spoil Bormann's plans now. He knew he would do no such thing as contact Hanna Reitsch. He avoided the communication room, at least for the moment. Instead, he went to his office, and pulled out the top drawer. His hand reached for his Luger pistol and a small vial of poison. He stuffed both inside his tunic and while Dr. Goebbels and some army officers were milling in the passageway, Bormann edged past them. He re-entered the room and saw Hitler at the far end. Bormann locked the door behind him quietly and carefully, so that Hitler would not notice.

"That was fast. Well?" Hitler asked. "Did you wire her?"

Bormann chose to remain silent. He bent over the radio by the sofa, and turned it up. Then he walked up to Hitler, until they were toe to toe.

"Well!" Hitler repeated, louder.

Bormann withdrew his Luger and aimed it at Hitler's face.

They stared each other down.

"What is this?" Hitler demanded.

"They call it a gun, you fool. I should have done this a long time ago."

Hitler's face grew flushed. "I could call the guards in and have you shot, Bormann."

"You do, and you'll die on the spot. Everyone will take it as a suicide."

Hitler scowled, hands on his hips. "So what are you waiting for? Pull the trigger."

"Not until I speak my mind."

"So, speak it."

178

Bormann took a breath. He'd been waiting a long time for this opportunity. "You let the country down, mein Fuehrer. You blew it, as the Americans would say."

"I let the—"

"Shut up! All you had to do was play along with the people who financed you. We all would have made money: our movement, the overseas banks, the oil companies, and we in Berlin would have remained in power. But no, you had to start a war that none of us wanted. The people, the military, the Party—none of us. Then you went ahead and had to start a two-front war by marching into Russia. You didn't learn any lessons from Napoleon's defeat, did you? You refused to retreat at any time. The British retreated at Dunkirk so that they could live to fight us another day. You didn't listen to your generals, who know a lot more than you do about tactics. Your military strategy cost us the war. You're a puffed-up imbecile." Bormann paused to see Hitler's face a beet red.

"Are you done?"

"No, I'm not done. You declared war on the United States when you didn't have to. In case you didn't figure it out, it was the Japanese that attacked the Americans. Not us. You did Roosevelt a favour. You had to liquidate millions, for which I and others will be blamed. Now the rest of us will all be on the run because of you. I detest you. I'm sick to death of you. You, and your damn chocolates. Too bad you didn't do us a favour and choke on one of them. And now you tell me you want to live. You're a monster. Any last words, Adolf?"

Hitler's nostrils flared. "I see it all now. You're a coward, hiding behind me all these years. All these papers I've been signing—I don't know what they are anymore. You're a back-stabber, a night crawler, a controller of bank accounts. You've been drugging me. I'm sure you have. You're the one who wants all the power, not Goering, or Himmler. It's you. I believe Goering now. You. . . you. . . You are a kiss-ass. A boot-licker. A skirt—"

Before Hitler could finish the word *skirt-chaser,* Bormann shot him in the temple. The blast propelled Hitler backwards into the chair behind him. "Rot in hell, you pig," Bormann whispered. He heard knocks at the door. Off to his right, Eva suddenly appeared at the sound of the shots. She stood frozen, too shocked to speak.

"As for you, you bitch," Bormann grunted. He grabbed her, and in one deft motion shoved the vial down her throat. He held her jaw closed and crunched her teeth to break the poison. She tried to spit it out, but couldn't. Bormann was too strong. In seconds, her eyes closed and she went limp in his arms. His wicked deed done, Bormann eased Hitler's wife to a nearby chair. He left Hitler where he was, the Luger on the floor beside him. Then Bormann walked to the door and opened it. The first person Bormann saw was Propaganda Minister Goebbels.

Bormann put on his best horrified face for him and the throng of military officers rushing up in the passageway. "They did it," he said, "right in front of me. The Fuehrer shot himself and Eva took poison. Let me out. There, there they are. I need some air. I'll be back to help."

The men pushed past Bormann to see for themselves.

Bormann still had tasks to perform. At his office, he called Else Krueger over. "That gunshot you heard was the Fuehrer. He killed himself. Eva took poison."

Krueger began to cry, softly.

Ignoring her, Bormann wrote out a message on a slip of paper.

Grand Admiral Doenitz:

In place of the former Reichmarshall Goering the Fuehrer appoints you as his successor. Written authority is on its way. You will immediately take all such measures as the situation requires.

"Send this to Doenitz's office," Bormann advised Krueger, touching her wrist. "At once."

She wiped her tears. "Yes, Herr Reichsleiter."

He looked up at his secretary. "Don't worry. Do your duty," he encouraged her.

She seemed to cheer up. "Yes, Herr Reichsleiter. But how can we go on without the Fuehrer?"

"We'll have to."

Bormann returned to Hitler's apartment to help a guard carry Eva's body into the pot-holed Chancellery courtyard. Behind the Reichsleiter, two guards had Hitler's remains wrapped in a blanket. At 3:30 in the afternoon, Hitler and Eva were set down beside each other in a pre-dug trench. Two guards doused the corpses with gasoline. "Stand back," Bormann said. He lit a newspaper and threw it on the bodies, while he and those handful present raised their right arms in a final and parting Nazi salute. In their last day on earth, Hitler was fifty-six, Eva was thirty-three. The man who had started the Second World War, the murderer of millions, had met his end.

Shielding himself from the high, overpowering flames with his arm, Goebbels said, loud enough for the crowd to hear, "It's every man. . . and woman, for himself now."

Twenty-seven

With the bodies still burning, a confirmed report of Hitler's death reached the OSS over shortwave. Allen Dulles trusted the source. Tom McCreedy and Wesley Hollinger were packed and on a train to the Swiss-German border by seven o'clock that evening. Next stop, Wernher von Braun and his brilliant team of scientists in the Thuringia Mountains. If they were still alive.

McCreedy drank from his glass of wine, seated inside their own compartment, the wheels clanking on the metal roadbed beneath them. "We haven't heard anything about Goebbels or Bormann. You know, that Goebbels, the Propaganda Minister, now there's someone people can learn from for the future. The OSS has conducted a study on him, how he uses media manipulation—radio, television, newspaper—to further his cause. Control the media, control the masses."

"You drink too much, Tom." Hollinger was on his first glass of wine. McCreedy was already on his third. And they had only been on the train an hour.

McCreedy laughed, cleaning his glasses with a handkerchief. "So you keep telling me, old buddy." He paused, and said, "When are you going to wake up and smell the roses."

"What do you mean?" Hollinger asked, his eyes on the breath-taking mountain scenery beyond the glass.

"We got lots of time, so you listen. You get both shotgun blasts this time."

Hollinger glanced at his sidekick. "More of this trading with the enemy stuff?"

"Other things."

"Like what?"

"Listen up. Hitler stepped out of line, and had to be brought down by the people—the international bankers—who had supported him financially. He was a risk. Many of those bankers, at least some, are Jews. Ironic, isn't it. Jews. Jews supporting Hitler. It's true. The Warburg family, for one. Filthy rich for hundreds of years, going back to Europe. Germany. The family is partners in Kuhn, Loeb, & Company, a New York banking house. They also represent the Rothschilds, who I'm sure you've heard of. "

"Yeah, I have."

"Worth billions. Not millions. *Billions!*" McCreedy let the word roll off his tongue. "Also Jews," McCreedy continued. "Nathan Rothschild once said, 'Give me the right to issue a nation's money, and then I do not care who makes its laws.' That's why Roosevelt never really had any power, only what was handed down to him from the super rich who control the economy. Truman, no different. He'll find out soon enough who wags his tail."

Hollinger thought back to February, Roosevelt at Yalta. The president admitted there were bigger forces at work than him. *'Bigger than me, that's what.'* Damn, maybe this McCreedy knew something after all.

"Anyway, getting back to Paul Warburg, he was one of the founding members of the U.S. Federal Reserve System in 1913, the same system that controls the American money supply to this day. Let me tell you now that our money is in the hands of private businessmen who disguise the Federal Reserve as a government agency. There was only one reason why the Fed was started."

"I've heard some things about the Fed. What do you think?"

"Wall Street bankers had to eliminate the competition. Or at least get them to knuckle under. The privately-owned banks across the country, that's who. Did you know that sixty percent of American banks were privately-owned in 1911?"

"No, I did not."

"At a secret meeting in 1911 on a Georgian island owned by the Morgans, representatives of several important Wall Street banks met to decide how they would get their hands on the U.S. Treasury. Seven men, who controlled one-quarter of the world's wealth. Filthy rich pricks who sought, and accomplished their objective. A central bank to dominate the bank reserves of the country. Men working for the Rockefellers, the Morgans, the Rothschilds in Europe. The Federal Reserve is a banking cartel in private hands, made to appear it's a government treasury. And it was some of these same seven—if not all—who lent money to the Nazi cause. Money out of our American treasury, technically. They also set up the Allies. You can't lose in a war if you support both sides. You can't beat these guys. They have all the marbles. You know," McCreedy said, sighing, "people think I'm crazy when I tell them this stuff. Am I getting through to you?"

"Sort of," Hollinger replied, recalling what Bill Donovan had told him four years ago about the Federal Reserve.

"You told me yourself that I.S. Filberg was receiving Wall Street loans for their munitions factories. Now, I'll tell you more. The objective of this group linked into a secret society with other prominent people around the world, is, one, an eventual one-world government. Two, universal army. That's why the League of Nations sprang up in the 1930s, although it failed, and that's why there's talk of a United Nations after the war. Three, a universal tax. And, four, a universal dictator, just as the Bible says. The Antichrist. Hitler failed at that. He wasn't the right guy for this New World Order. The banking group spawned Hitler to keep Germany from going under after the First Great War, when inflation was soaring, then canned him when he went too far. He was biting the hand that was feeding him. The Jewish bankers didn't support his mistreatment of their race."

"Let it be," Hollinger said, but not convincingly.

"You have to think globally, Wesley. Here, I'll show you something. Take out a dollar bill."

"What for?"

"OK." McCreedy withdrew an American one dollar from his wallet and waved it in front of Hollinger. "On the other side of George Washington is this symbol on the left side, here. The pyramid and all-seeing eye."

Hollinger looked over. "So?"

"Below it reads a Latin phrase, *Novus Ordo Seclorum*, which translated is New World Order. Global thinking, my friend, that's the future. You'll see. Countries around the world will be so linked by this superrich race of bankers that when the next wars come along, no one will know who the enemy really is because each country will be financed by the same people on the enemy's side. Do you get what I'm saying? In fact, a lot of wars might not even start because no country will be operating its own treasury. It will be controlled by foreign investors, as is the case in this war."

Hollinger rubbed his face. "Geez, Tom, this is too much."

"OK, off topic a bit, who do you think foots the bill for Communism?"

"Wall Street, too?"

"You're right. One of the partners in the Kuhn, Loeb & Company that I already mentioned—his name was Jacob Schiff—was one of the main backers of the Bolshevik Revolution of 1917. How? He loaned money to Leon Trotsky for his good-will tour of the United States looking for support. As soon as Lenin's boys overthrew the Czars, all the banks in the country were nationalized, except for a National City Bank in Petrograd."

"Rockefeller," Hollinger said automatically.

"Then Standard Oil rigs—also owned by Rockefeller—moved into the Soviet Union to set up business. Loans were provided through—"

"The National City Bank."

McCreedy threw his hands up. "Now you're with me. And I'll tell you something else, if it wasn't for Germany's Junkers Aircraft, there never would have been any Soviet air power in this war. A British company, Lena Goldfields, has been mining ore in Siberia for decades, and using slave labour. American companies are mining Russian manganese and asbestos. Shortly after Lenin took power, the Wilson Administration sent almost a billion tons of emergency food to the Soviet Union or else the country would have starved."

"How did we get onto the Communists? Let's stick to Germany."

"OK. Let's see, when Hitler was looking for support in America during his rise to power, I.S. Filberg, the German cartel, hired the public relations firm of Ivy Lee to help improve Hitler's image. This was the same firm used by old man John D. Rockefeller, when his very own image went sour. And, you know, this sort of thing went on years ago, even in the Civil War. The Rothschilds bankrolled both and North and South, through an agent they had sent over from England."

Hollinger shut his eyes. "Wait, wait! How the hell do you know all this stuff?" he demanded.

"You have to dig for it. Old newspapers. I know people. Thanks to my government access, which I often abuse, I've seen files."

Hollinger finished off his glass of wine. The train took a wide turn through a mountain pass, and all he saw, when he glanced over, was a giant wall of dark rock. "What about our present situation? If all this, what you're telling me, is true, then why are we racing to get to the German scientists before the Russians? I thought we're supposed to be one big, happy family?"

"The rich group will still supply a new and bigger enemy than the Nazis along the way, simply because there'll be huge profits in it for them, financing both sides. Global opposites is profitable for military build-up. Two great forces in the world will both be directed by the same powerful boardroom. Two forces, one master. The war was fought to preserve Communism for their financial benefit."

"The Russians?" Hollinger sat up, interested.

McCreedy waved his finger at Hollinger, and raised his voice, "Who else? They will be the next world power. Hell, they've taken half of Europe away from Hitler already. They won't give it back. An arms race is the next thing. Money has to be made. The same way that they cause wars. The group live by the saying, 'when there's blood in the streets, there's profit in the boardroom.' "

Hollinger removed his suit jacket, placing it on the couch beside him. "I wouldn't mind some sleep before we reach the border."

"Too much for you, eh?

"Yeah," Hollinger sighed. "Let's concentrate on our mission. So, it's all set, is it, at the border?"

"Yeah. All we have to do is clear through customs, which shouldn't be much of a problem because Patton's Third Army is in charge of most border points from here to Austria."

Hollinger shut his eyes and wondered whether, if McCreedy was right, the world was going all to hell.

Twenty-eight

The two OSS agents made it to the Austrian-German border after midnight. There to meet them and take them into Germany was a tall, husky army officer, with a flashlight in his hand and a long cigar in his mouth. Crowded around him was a seasoned detachment of twenty-five gun-toting young men, their uniforms worn from battle.

"Welcome to Germany. I'm Colonel Burns. 324th Infantry Regiment, 44th U.S. Infantry Division. You must be Hollinger and McCreedy."

"We are," Hollinger answered.

"You got ID?"

"Yes, sir," Hollinger said, flashing his OSS identification the same time McCreedy did.

Burns shone the flashlight at the cards, and seemed convinced. "You can't go anywhere dressed like that." The colonel looked over his shoulder at a junior officer. "Parker?"

A lieutenant stepped forward. "Yes, sir."

"Get these men some army gear and pistols. And find some kit bags for their civvies."

"Yes, sir, colonel."

"You men do know how to handle hardware, do you?"

"Yes, we do," McCreedy answered.

Burns smiled at Hollinger. "By the way, where do you get your suit? I haven't seen one like that since I left the States."

"Custom-made in England."

"Nice tie."

"Thanks."

"Kind of bright, though. OK, the situation. Over here." Burns spread out a map on the fender of a jeep. "Help me out with another flashlight, Parker." Under two lights, Burns explained: "We're here. Mittenwald. Last we heard, the scientists were at Oberammergau. There. Twenty miles."

"A set of army barracks, right?"

"That's right, Mr. Hollinger. Guarded by SS troops."

"Do we expect trouble?"

Burns shrugged. "It's possible, even though it's now confirmed that Hitler is deader than a hammer. Either they'll give up or fight to the end for the Fuehrer. Who knows? But we're prepared for anything."

Hollinger glanced around. "It seems you are."

"If we need any more men, we'll get them," Burns assured the OSS agents.

HOHENLYCHEN

Himmler took the dispatch delivered to him by courier from the office of Admiral Doenitz. Himmler read it, then crumpled it in his hand. Dammit. He was dismissed forthwith from all his posts. He removed his glasses and rubbed his sore eyes. Lately, he was prone to stomach cramps, headaches, and terrible dreams. Today was no exception. He stood, slowly, his forty-five-year-old body aching him with every move.

He strode to the washroom aboard his train and lathered his moustache before the mirror. Through the window, he saw his adjutant and two male secretaries throwing files in the bonfire, the flames shooting eight feet high into the afternoon sky. After all these years, this is what it had come to. Destroy everything. Himmler knew that all German forces had more than likely pledged allegiance to Doenitz. The deposed SS and Gestapo chief didn't stand a chance now. Without power, and without any verbal contact with the SS guards in Bavaria, his collateral was gone. Never mind the scientists, anyway. Himmler figured that the guards had probably deserted their posts as soon as they heard Hitler was dead. That meant no peace terms with Eisenhower or Montgomery looming on the horizon.

When Himmler emerged from the washroom, his face was clean-shaven, and he had two vials of instant-acting cyanide in the trouser pocket of his civilian clothing. He found the file incriminating Martin

Bormann as Hitler's messenger of mass murder, and took the sheets out. He walked outside, threw his diary into the fire, then stopped in front of Ludwig Hahn to shake his hand. He only glanced approvingly at the other men. Himmler walked to his limousine, door open, his driver waiting. His subordinates were left to fend for themselves.

"Switzerland," Himmler said in a trance to his driver, as he stuffed the sheets incriminating Bormann inside his shirt.

Berlin

Martin Bormann was not in the mood to celebrate his forty-fifth birthday. He was the last of the Nazi high command left in the Fuehrerbunker. Only two army generals and some officers remained below. An hour before in the pot-holed Chancellery garden, Goebbels had shot himself, and his wife, Magda, had swallowed poison, their six children already dead from the same batch of lethal cyanide. Like Hitler and Eva, their bodies too were doused with petrol and set aflame. No longer interested in living, the last thing Dr. Goebbels wanted for his family was *to be brought up in a non-National Socialist Germany.*

Bormann had other plans for his hide. He had a distinct advantage over the other Nazi brass. Hardly photographed throughout his rise to power on Hitler's coattails, neither the Russians nor most Germans could identify him on sight, especially now in civilian clothing.

He and Else Krueger walked up the stairs hand-in-hand to the bunker entrance. On the surface, machine guns rattled and heavy artillery pounded in the night. He stamped out his cigarette on the top stair. The Fuehrer had hated smoking in the bunker. Bormann had already said his goodbyes to his other secretaries, the ones he had fondled at work or slept with over the years. Bormann stopped Else at the second step, and said with passion, "Goodbye, Else. Good luck. Women will not be safe out there." He kissed her hand with intent. "I always, and I mean always, had the greatest amount of respect for you."

They hugged.

She managed a weak smile. "Goodbye, Martin. Happy birthday."

It was the first time they had used each other's first names.

"Thank you. Too bad there's no time to celebrate. Be brave." He gave her a loaded Luger, and in a soft voice said, "Don't worry, I have another. Use it, if you have to."

Bormann left first.

As soon as he stepped through the unguarded entrance, he was fired at by a sniper. The bullets pinged off the concrete. He could not tell where the shots were coming from. Bormann ducked off to the right, and dove for a pile of rubble a few feet away. He saw Else leaving, her shadowy figure keeping down, running in the opposite direction, even more bullets pinging at her. Obviously, the Russians were monitoring the bunker. Bormann backed up, squatted down, and ran through the water-puddled Chancellery garden, past the bodies of Dr. Goebbels, Magda, Eva, and Hitler, to the street beyond the crumbled walls, the flames of the still-burning Goebbels family lighting the way. He stopped behind a pile of bricks in front of the subway station, and bent over to catch his breath. There was no electricity in Berlin, but several large fires brightened the sky. He knew this was going to be tough. It would require a lot of luck and a good lot of running to escape the city through the Russian lines. He should have kept in better shape. Maybe some of Hitler's chocolates would fire him up. Bormann chuckled to himself at that thought. What a time to think of chocolates.

He slowly entered the subway station. This was his only escape on such short notice. He would crawl through the many tunnels, then, once outside, he would walk along the tracks until he reached the Friedrichstrasse Station, a few hundred yards away, where the only German fighting men left were still holding off the Russian onslaught. They were the three-thousand strong Battle Group Mohnke, a rag-tag outfit of sailors, paratroopers, Hitler Youths, and SS men. A few hundred yards from the station stood the Weidendammer Bridge over the Spree River, and a possible escape through Berlin's north-western suburbs.

Bormann withdrew his Luger from his leather overcoat. Holding it waist high, he stepped forward into uncertainty.

Some birthday.

Twenty-nine

Magnus Von Braun left the army barracks on a bicycle, riding in the direction of the American army. He spoke and understood the English language quite well, and because of that he was the one chosen from the team of scientists to make contact with the Americans.

It was a sunny morning, a few clouds in the sky. Magnus peddled for a few miles along a winding, gravel road, thick with pine trees to either side. He heard something. He drew to a halt by the side of the road, a bend ahead blocking his view. They were trucks. Drawing closer. But were they American? Or German? Or worse—Russian?

He dove for cover in the ditch, taking the bicycle with him.

In the lead jeep was Hollinger, McCreedy, Lieutenant Parker, and Colonel Burns. Hollinger pointed as the jeep roared around the bend. "Did you see that?" he said, from the back seat.

"Yeah, I did," said Parker, behind the wheel.

Colonel Burns puffed on a fresh cigar in the front. "Me, too. Somebody leaped into the bushes. Pull up here."

The jeep's brakes squealed. All four had their pistols at the ready. Burns held his hand up for the six jeeps behind him to stop.

"Easy," Burns said, his voice barely audible, stepping out onto the gravel. "Parker, you go that way to the left. I'll go right. Hollinger, you go with Parker. McCreedy, you—" Burns didn't have to go any further. A blonde-haired man popped up from the ditch, slowly dragging the bicycle towards them, coming to a dead stop thirty feet away from the jeep.

Burns turned behind him and quickly said, "You know German, Hollinger. Tell him to come forward with his hands up."

Hollinger slipped out from the others. "Komm vorwarts mit die Haende boch!" He yelled.

The man dropped his bicycle and raised his hands. "Americans. You are Americans."

"You speak English?" Burns asked.

"Yes, I do," the smiling man replied, walking up to them. Parker searched him for weapons as he continued talking. "My brother and I have been trying to find you for days."

"He's clean," Parker said.

"Why?" Burns wanted to know.

"We need your help."

"Who are you? What's your name?"

"Magnus von Braun."

"Brother to Wernher von Braun?"

"Yes."

"Put your hands down."

"Thank you."

Hollinger smiled at McCreedy. They had hit paydirt.

McCreedy laughed. "Are we lucky or what? Are you one of the scientists?"

Magnus nodded. "Yes."

Hollinger was puzzled. "How did you get away from the SS?"

"Oh, they took off for who knows where when the news came through that Adolf Hitler had died. I was elected as spokesman, since my English is the best."

"It sure is. Where are the rest? We've come for you."

"We had to split up," Magnus said. "We were all ordered by the SS to the army barracks at Oberammergau. After a few days, my brother convinced the SS that he and his team should be dispersed so that we wouldn't all be wiped out in one air strike, should your planes decide to drop bombs on the barracks. They agreed."

"So where are they?" Hollinger asked.

"At Oberjoch."

"The SS with them?"

"I do not know that. But probably not."

"So, you don't know if they're alive, even?"

Magnus shrugged. "No, not with any certainty."

Burns swung around at his lieutenant. "Parker? Where's Oberjoch?"

Parker opened his map on the jeep hood. "Just a few miles from here, along this road. We'll be there in a few minutes."

"Are you people in good health?" Burns's gaze fell on Magnus.

"Yes, very much so. A little hungry."

"We'll look after you," Burns promised.

"Thank you. You'll have to excuse my brother, though. He's still healing from a broken arm he suffered when he had to leave Peenemunde. His driver had fallen asleep and banged into a tree."

Hollinger had to ask the question. "The blueprints and documents on your research, do you have them?"

"Yes. At an abandoned mine near Dornten. Two of my brother's aides hid them there and blasted the tunnel shut."

"Where's Dornten?"

"In the Harz Mountains."

"That's in Thuringia," Parker piped up. "Colonel," he glanced down at the map, "the Russians are moving in that region."

"*Colonel.*" Hollinger said.

"I know, Hollinger. We'll get them," Burns assured the OSS agent. "Are these aides with your group at Oberammergau?"

"One is. The other is with Wernher."

"What are we waiting for?" Burns said. "Let's move it." By now, most of the jeep drivers had gathered around. "Follow me, men. Mr. von Braun, lead the way to your army barracks."

"I would be glad to."

BERLIN

Bormann still hadn't escaped the capital. Over the last twenty-four hours since he had fled the Fuehrerbunker, he had made it safely to the Friedrichstrasse subway station, one of the few areas in Berlin that remained in German hands, for the moment. Battle Group Mohnke was putting up a fight against their Red Army counterparts. In this German-held pocket, Bormann had watched the fighting for most of the day from the shadows of a dusty, bombed-out warehouse near the Weidendammer Bridge.

At night, he ventured out from his hideaway, staying low. He made his way along the Spree River, in the direction of the northwest suburbs, using brick rubble as a shield against Russian snipers. Downstream, he had found a spot where large concrete chunks of buildings had been thrown into the river enough so that he could walk across. But what was on the other side? No matter, he had to try.

Bormann reached the other side safely in the darkness and rested until morning, then set out on foot away from the Spree River, the thud of small arms behind him. The only faces he saw belonged to forlorn Germans. Not a Russian in sight. By now, Hitler's former secretary was used to the dreary sight of war. Still, the damage and the waste brought on by the Fuehrer disturbed him. It was strange how immune he once was to the reality of war, stowed away with the Fuehrer wherever he went, be it Berchtesgaden, or the Chancellery, or the bunker. After an hour he saw houses ahead, a residential district, mostly untouched by shellfire. He was in the suburbs that led out of the city, and hopefully clean away from the Red Army. He stopped by the side of a stone house, opposite a tree and slouched down for another rest. He was truly lucky, so far. Leaning his head back, he licked his lips. He was thirsty and tired.

He closed his eyes for a moment and drifted off. . .

Then he was nudged awake by a young, dirty Russian soldier. Bormann stood to his feet. The Russian grinned at him. What was he doing alone? Were there other soldiers in the vicinity? Bormann didn't wish to wait around to find out. He quickly kicked the legs out from the soldier, and fired his Luger into the man's chest.

Twice.

Thirty

They were part of a special unit known as Jet Propulsion Section, Research and Intelligence Branch, Army Ordnance Technical Division, commanded by Major Robert Staver. McCreedy, Hollinger, and the two von Braun brothers watched as two U.S. Army sergeants lugged in the half-dozen crates of documents down the wooden steps and into the cellar of the three-story house.

As soon as the men departed, Magnus popped open the lid of each one. Pleased with what he saw at first glance, he nodded at his brother, whom he was interpreting for. Wernher von Braun, his arm in a sling, smiled. The paperwork appeared to be in order. Apparently, Staver's men did well, digging the crates out of the abandoned mine in Thuringia only days before the Russian Red Army took over that area of Germany.

"Does it look like we have everything?" Hollinger asked.

"It seems that way, yes," Magnus said, answering for his brother.

"The V-4's?"

"Right here, Mr. Hollinger. In the middle of this first box." Magnus rummaged through one crate and showed the OSS agents a two-inch thick file pertaining to the Foo Fighter.

"Geez!" McCreedy exclaimed, zipping through the technical pages. "Look at this will you."

"I'm looking," Hollinger said.

"*Projekt Equinox*, Mr. McCreedy and Mr. Hollinger. Of course, we do have other projects for your pleasure. Lasers, V-2's, research on space travel, the sky is the limit, as Wernher has often told me."

197

"A little pun there, right?" McCreedy added, smirking.

"A what?"

"*Gentlemen!*"

At the foot of the steps stood an officer. His hands behind his back.

"Who are you?" Hollinger spoke out.

The officer approached, confidently. He was average height, on the thin side, in his forties. "General Lomax, United States Army Air Force. I have been given the authority to commandeer all data pertaining to *Project Equinox.*"

"Says who?" Hollinger barked.

"The President of the United States and the Office of Strategic Services. That's who. Here is my documentation."

Hollinger opened the envelope passed to him.

"Damn, this thing is signed by Donovan. And Truman."

"Yes, sir."

Hollinger showed one of the pages to McCreedy.

"That's Donovan's signature, all right," McCreedy said. "What gives?"

"Well, what do you know," Hollinger frowned. "After all the time I've spent on this, weeks away from home, the Army Air Force is taking over the V-4 file." Hollinger should not have been surprised. With Roosevelt gone, Truman in, there was a power shift in Washington. A changing of the guard.

"This is now a classified project," Lomax insisted, taking the papers out of Hollinger's hand. "Do not discuss it with anyone."

"I know. I know. I've been there before."

McCreedy grunted. "Since when does the Air Force tell the OSS what to do?"

General Lomax folded his arms across his chest. "Since now."

BAVARIA, GERMANY—MAY 8

American troops found Reichmarshall Hermann Goering on a congested road the day the war was officially announced over. They pulled him from his limousine and took him off to a local interrogation centre. He and his entourage of nurse, doctor, and adjutant were in good humour, especially Goering, who was treated as a celebrity.

Goering had wanted to surrender to the Americans after his SS captors released him three days earlier to fend for himself. At a hastily called press conference that afternoon, in the open air behind the inter-rogation centre, he was asked several questions in German.

"You know that Hitler and Goebbels are dead, do you not?" one reporter stood and asked.

Goering stayed seated, squinting in the bright sunshine. "Yes, of course I do."

"Do you know the whereabouts of Heinrich Himmler?"

"I do not. I don't care where he is."

"Were you and Himmler friends?"

"No."

"When did you see him last?"

"At Hitler's bunker in Berlin. April 20th. It was a party for Hitler's birthday."

"Was that the last time you saw Hitler?"

"Yes."

"Were you asked to be Hitler's successor?"

"No."

"Did you try to take power on your own?"

Goering felt a chill, despite the sun's warmth. "I thought about it."

"Where's Martin Bormann?" a different reporter asked.

Goering cleared his throat. He knew now that he never should have collaborated with Bormann on anything. For all he knew, Bormann might have gotten away and was now lying on a tropical beach some-where. Then again. . . Goering, on the other hand, had nothing left. No money. At least not in Germany. Only his Swiss bank accounts, which he couldn't access. No V-4 blueprints. They were taken from him by the SS, who found them on his person. No Luftwaffe to command. No power.

Goering let the audience fall quiet. Then his lips began to move, slowly. "I hope that Martin Bormann is burning in hell, because that's exactly what he deserves."

LONDON

Hollinger wished he had picked a better day to return to London. The town was celebrating. Shouting, drinking, dancing. The war was over. People clogged the streets. It took him hours to get from the airport to his apartment building, a trip that should have taken forty or fifty minutes at most.

He climbed the steps, opened the door, and saw Roberta sitting on the couch.

She looked up, open-mouthed, as if she had seen a ghost. "Wesley, where the hell have you been?"

"Here and there. What kind of greeting is that?"

They ran for each other and embraced.

"Now, that's better," he said, kissing her. "You're bigger. And your stomach's in the way." He poked her with his finger. "You look. . . well done."

Three days later, nine-pound, two-ounce Wesley Hollinger, Jr. was born to proud parents.

"Congratulations," London's OSS Director said. He and Hollinger were sitting in comfortable lobby chairs outside the maternity section.

"Thank you, sir. Cigar? But don't smoke it in here."

"I won't." Jack Dorwin took the cigar, dropping it into his inside suit jacket. "Thanks."

"You're welcome. So, did you find Bormann?" Hollinger asked, his voice low.

"Hell, no. The guy disappeared. No sign of him at the bunker, nor anywhere in Berlin. Not yet, anyway. Donovan and Dulles sure want him bad."

"So I've heard."

"The only news I got is that he left Hitler's bunker on the first of May, only hours before the Red Army took the Chancellery. And hasn't been seen since."

"Any contact with his Swiss banking friends?"

"Nothing that they admit to."

"The scientists?"

"That's why I'm here. Wesley, I have some other news for you. I don't know if you're going to like it. Orders from Donovan."

Hollinger slouched in his chair. "Where are they sending me this time?"

"How'd you guess?"

"I have this sixth sense. Where, sir?"

"Washington. After Roberta gets back on her feet."

"Please, sir, let's not rush it. She's had a rough time of it lately."

"I'll hold Donovan off."

"Thank you. So what will I be doing?

"A new assignment under *Operation Paperclip*. Donovan will fill you in. I don't know anything about it myself, only that the scientists will fall into it. I can say this, too. There's some big changes ahead for the OSS."

"What kind of changes?"

Dorwin smiled. "You'll see." He stood. "So, can I pop in on Roberta and the baby now?"

"Sure," Hollinger said, thinking of Washington instead.

It was back to the States. This time with a wife and baby.

Thirty-one

While Rudolf Hess, Hermann Goering and Albert Speer, and scores of other Nazis stood trial at Nuremberg for war crimes, a small band of fanatic Nazis were toasting a new pro-German regime, thousands of miles away in an elaborate Argentine mountain chalet high in the Andes.

"To the Fourth Reich," the ex-submariner Manfred Stoeller said, hoisting his glass out at arm's length.

"To the Fourth Reich," the group of men joined in with enthusiastic voices. The six of them drank their schnapps. Like Stoeller, all were escapees from their Fatherland before it went under in May, 1945. Two men were SS concentration camp commandants. Another two were army generals. One used to be a Berlin doctor who had been on Heinrich Himmler's Gestapo payroll. Stoeller's story was unique. When Germany capitulated, he had taken to the open sea off northern Germany in a stolen submarine with a skeleton staff, who were presently splintered across South America. Refuelled in Spain, Stoeller had made it safely to the shores of Argentina. It was that easy. The five others in the group today had more hair-raising tales to tell. All had one thing in common. They had money socked away in bank accounts around the world, ready for future use.

"May this Reich survive," Stoeller continued. Smiling, he said, "Now, the initiation." Handed a copy of Hitler's *Mein Kampf* by one of the army generals, Stoeller motioned at the Berlin doctor. A circle formed. "Doctor Straff."

"Yes, Herr Stoeller."

"With your left hand on the divine word, you will read the oath from the sheet, please," Stoeller advised, holding a typed piece of paper for the doctor.

Straff, in his forties, wore a thick moustache over a tanned face. He took the sheet and began:

I, Doctor Walter Straff, of my own free will and accord, and under the threat of my own death, solemnly and sincerely swear that I will always secretly hail and henceforth never reveal the cherished mysteries of the Order of the Knights of National Socialism and our ruler, the Commander Fuehrer, to the profane, those who are not chosen to stand by us in our global struggle. I furthermore promise and swear that I will protect any and every fellow blood brother of the Order of the Knights of National Socialism from the profane who seek to pervert or destroy our hallowed Order, so help me the most excellent and worshipful lord of this world. Hail Commander Fuehrer and his divine wisdom."

Stoeller snatched the sheet from Straff, as he had done to Otto Bauer off the coast of Greenland more than a year before. Stoeller then said, "Doctor Walter Straff, you are now a brother to the first degree of the Order of the Knights of National Socialism. Welcome to the elite fraternity."

Straff glanced around at the faces in the circle. "Thank you. I am honoured."

The other five members of the Order bowed, clicking their heels.

Stoeller handed Straff his gold Order medallion, and his bright red sash, embroidered with a black swastika inside a white circle. "Wear them on your person when you meet secretly with other brothers in the Order."

"I will." Straff cleared his throat. "May I ask a question blood brother, Herr Stoeller?"

"Yes, certainly."

"It is because I am inquisitive."

"Go ahead, please."

"Who is the Commander Fuehrer, now that Hitler is dead?"

A slight twinkle sparked Stoeller's eyes. "We thought you'd never ask. Come with me to the balcony, please."

Together, the two walked the length of the room, stopping opposite the French doors. Sitting on the other side of the glass was a powerfully built man with a receding hairline, casually studying the mountain scenery through binoculars. He leaned on the round table in front of him. He was wearing some kind of uniform that was unfamiliar to Straff. The man's boots shone like diamonds in the sun. Stoeller opened the door, and stepped out into the cool mountain air. The man didn't move.

"Commander Fuehrer, we have sworn in another member of the Order."

The man stood and turned around, slowly. His legs spread out. He was not tall by any means, and about the same age as he was, the doctor noticed. He had seen the man somewhere before. But where? That uniform was unusual. The breeches, the boots, the tunic. It was not SS. It was not Gestapo. It definitely wasn't a military service uniform. That face. That *round* face. The uniform was that of a Reichsleiter. Not too many of those in the old Nazi regime. Then it hit him. Straff had only seen the man once before, at a Nazi Party rally in Berlin, 1937. But wasn't he *presumed dead* by authorities? Straff recalled the recent newsreels he had seen, taken outside the bunker. The charred bodies. Hitler. Eva Braun. Goebbels, his wife, and his children.

Stoeller stood ramrod straight. "Doctor Straff, meet the Commander Fuehrer of the Order of the Knights of National Socialism."

"Bormann?"

"Yes."

"I mean, Herr Bormann?"

"Yes, it's me." Martin Bormann set his binoculars on the table. "Pleased to make your acquaintance, Doctor Straff. Welcome to the Order."

Straff's expression displayed a combination of horror and amusement. "But Herr Bormann, how did you ever get out of Berlin? Did the Russians not have the city surrounded?"

"They did. But I got through."

"How did you get off the continent?"

Bormann smiled for the first time. "It wasn't easy, Herr Doctor Straff. It wasn't easy."

At a newsstand after an easy day at the office, Wesley Hollinger Sr. bought a copy of the *Washington Post* and took it home to his suburban Arlington, Virginia bungalow with the paved driveway and the wide front lawn. He lived in a neighbourhood of other Washington working-class people. He was a family man now. Wife, kid, mortgage.

Hollinger's old employer, the OSS, was no more. Disbanded by President Harry Truman on October 1, 1945 by Executive Order 9621, a new peacetime organization was beginning to rise in its place, unofficially entitled the Central Intelligence Group for the moment. Hollinger's future position with them was still unclear, although he was presently an assistant to the Director of German Operations. His latest assignment was to monitor the recent reports of two Martin Bormann sightings in Argentina.

As he made his way through the door, Wesley Jr. ran for his father. Hollinger dropped the paper, picked his son up and twirled him over his head. "Hi, Wesley. How's my boy?" His son squealed and giggled.

After dinner that night, with his son in bed, Hollinger finally got a chance to read the paper. He took the sports section first to catch up on details of the World Series between the Boston Red Sox and the St. Louis Cardinals, which the Red Sox were leading three games to two. Roberta joined him in the library. His wife was now a teacher in a local high school, but still on the British Secret Service part-time pay sheets. "Once MI-6, always MI-6," she had been told by Colonel Lampert.

"Do you mind if I take a section?"

Hollinger looked around the side of the paper. He glanced down at the rest of the copy on the coffee table. "Go ahead," he smirked, then returned to his reading.

After a few moments, Roberta shrieked. "My God! Wesley!"

"What's the matter?"

"Tom McCreedy was found dead in his home, a suicide note by his bed."

"Get out!"

"Look for yourself."

Hollinger took the paper from his wife. He read the notice. "Geez, you're right."

"What would make him commit suicide?"

Hollinger slouched in his chair. He thought about that one. What indeed? McCreedy had just married that spring. He seemed happy at his new job with the intelligence organization as a financial assistant to the new National Director. "You know, he had once said to me that it was scary to know too much."

"Whatever do you mean?"

Hollinger rubbed his brow. "He was murdered. The idiot!"

"By whom?"

He handed her back the paper. "Honey, put on some tea."

"I already did. It should be ready."

"Good. My throat's dry. I have to tell you something."

Epilogue

Kenneth Arnold left the runway at Chehalis in his privately-owned
Piper Cub, bound for Seattle where he was to attend a meeting as a
representative for his employer, Fire Control Equipment Company of
Boise, Idaho.

It was a gorgeous day. The sun was shining. The sky was clear. No
haze. Very little turbulence. A great day to fly. That afternoon, only a
few minutes into the air, the thirty-two-year-old businessman caught
a magnificent view of the jutting, high peaks of the Cascade Range. No
worries, the trip did not bother Arnold, despite the fact that a Marine
Corp C-46 transport had crashed against the side of Mt. Rainier the
night before. He continued climbing, levelling off at nine thousand feet.
Flying to one side of scenic Mt. Rainier, he saw a quick flash to his left.
At first, he thought it was an explosion. He was wrong. Nine silvery
objects, resembling inverted plates, skimmed across the mountain
tops at incredible speed, and formed up in a chain-like line. Then he
wondered if they were the new American jet fighters that were coming
into service. Stretching across the sky for what he guessed was five
miles, they were gleaming in the sun, hovering, darting up and down.
These were not normal aircraft.

Approaching within a few miles, he determined that the machines
were solid objects, metallic and circular, about a hundred feet in diameter, with no rudder or tail section. The centre of each had a shiny
cupola. As Arnold drew nearer, the nine objects flew north at fantastic speeds from a standing stop, disappearing in seconds. Arnold was

spellbound. He decided to work out the mathematics. When the first aircraft shot past Mt. Rainier, his panel clock read exactly one minute to three. When the last object drew even with the crest of Mt. Adams, the elapsed time was one minute and 42 seconds. Arnold dug for his area map. The peaks were 47 miles apart. Sweat began to form on his face. According to his calculations, the speed had to be about 1,600 miles per hour!

How could that be!

When Arnold landed and told his story, reporters sought him out. "They flew like a saucer would if you skipped it across the water," he told the press. Many were doubtful.

Kenneth Arnold had coined a new phrase. The words "flying saucer" had come into being.

That week, at least twenty other people in widely scattered areas of the United States reported seeing similar shiny, fast-moving objects in the skies.

Afterword

Many characters in this novel are fictional, such as Wesley Hollinger, Roberta Langford-Hollinger, Raymond Lampert, Wilhelm Raeder, Manfred Stoeller, Tom McCreedy, Jack Dorwin, Otto Bauer, Benito Cocapo, Johanna Erickson, Art Tooney and Karl Zeller.

Argentina

A military junta led by Colonel Juan Peron seized power in 1945, placing General Arturo Rawson as president, although it was Peron who really ran the country. Peron, who supported Hitler earlier in the war, made himself president in 1946, and quickly fashioned his new state police after Heinrich Himmler's Gestapo. Argentina, along with other South American countries, became a safe haven for Nazi war criminals. A bloody revolt sent Peron into exile in September 1955.

Antarctica

It is a historical fact that German submariners used the waters and the northern edge for supply and fuelling stations. The British took permanent occupation of the peninsula in 1943 to observe enemy action. For the next decade, the British conducted aerial surveys and drew maps of the area. By 1958, several countries around the world began their own expeditions to the frozen continent.

Bilderbergers

This "one world" secret society of over one hundred members meet behind closed doors at a different spot in the world once a year to discuss how the world can become knitted closer together politically and economically.

The Bilderbergers are influential people who are in favour of UN military forces, Free Trade Agreements, and global thinking on such issues as peace, forestry, animal rights, and common currencies. Very few details, if any, of each meeting are leaked to the mainline press. Professor Carroll Quigley stated it best in his 1,300 page book, *Tragedy and Hope*, published in 1966. "Their aim is nothing less than to create a world system of financial control in private hands able to dominate the political system of each country and the economy of the world as a whole."

Martin Bormann

Did he get away? No one knows for sure. A so-called positive identification was made in 1998 of a body found in Berlin, if one can believe positive identifications anymore. His wife Magda died in March, 1946, all the time under close surveillance, while she waited for her husband to materialize. Bormann had never reached her, his final telegram from Berlin reading: "Everything is lost, I will never get out of here. Take care of the children."

Huge rewards were offered by post-war German governments and Jewish organizations for any information leading to his capture. Although the West German government officially declared him dead in 1973, author Ladislas Farago wrote the book *Aftermath*, published in 1974, with his proof that Martin Bormann had actually survived the war and was living out his final years in South America.

Winston Churchill

Despite his strong leadership of the British Empire through the war, the British voted him out of office in 1945, with the belief that he was great in war but would be lousy in peace time. Six years later, in 1951, the voters had a change of heart by returning him to office at age 76. He was knighted two years later, and died in 1965.

CIA

The Central Intelligence Agency replaced the OSS two years after the war ended.

Bill Donovan

The OSS disbanded, he bowed out of official intelligence work and returned to his New York law office. He died in 1959.

Allen Dulles
Returned to his law practice in New York until 1950, when he joined the CIA as Deputy Director for Plans, and Deputy Director of the CIA a year later. From 1953 to 1961, he was appointed by President Dwight Eisenhower as the Director of Central Intelligence, holding the top post until the CIA-backed Bay of Pigs fiasco, for which he was blamed, and was subsequently fired by President John F. Kennedy. He later served on the President's Commission on the Assassination of President Kennedy. It was this same committee that fostered the outlandish Magic Bullet Theory that today is considered a joke.

He died January 28, 1969, at the age of seventy-five.

Hermann Goering
Goering was found guilty of war crimes at Nuremberg in 1946 for his knowledge of the concentration camps and his association to the secret police. But he beat the hangman by taking poison before he was put to death.

Heinrich Himmler
While escaping to Switzerland in May 1945, he was rounded up with other suspects at an Allied checkpoint at Bremervorde, Germany. Taken to an interrogation centre nearby, he was identified by an American Army officer and immediately searched. However, Himmler swallowed a capsule of cyanide he had placed between his teeth, and although his captors tried to save his life by pumping his stomach, he died fifteen minutes later. It was not recorded if he had any files or papers on him.

Operation Paperclip
This was the clandestine Army-OSS-CIA intelligence operation used to bring Wernher von Braun and his talented group of scientists to the United States as "resident aliens." They immigrated without visas, but with the knowledge of President Truman. The files of those individuals who had been selected to come to the States from Germany were distinguished by paperclips.

George Patton
Patton constantly complained about General Eisenhower's war leadership. Once Germany was defeated, Patton wanted to take on the Russians. For such insubordination, he was relieved of his Third Army

Command in late 1945, with the idea that he was losing his mind. He died from complications following a traffic accident a few months later. It has been speculated since that Patton was actually assassinated by his own people. Some say he was considered a threat to European peace and Dwight Eisenhower's long-range plans for the presidency.

Trading with the enemy
With the weakening of the Freedom of Information Act in the late 1970s, files have been open to the public to show that American corporations such as Standard Oil, ITT, Ford, and Chase Bank, participated in financing the enemy during the Second World War, as mentioned in this novel. Scores of books have been published since to support these findings, with details on how the transactions were completed.

Wernher von Braun
Upon his arrival in the United States, he devoted his energies to space exploration, his first love, and was the founding father of NASA and the Apollo moon landings.

United States Air Force
The USAF came into being in 1947 as its own service, breaking away from the Army. They quickly took charge of evaluating all the thousands of UFO and Flying Saucer sightings, under *Project Blue Book*.

Flying Saucers
There were thousands more of these Unidentified Flying Object sightings in the United States, as well as around the world, between the years 1947-1952. The USAF made an intensive study of nearly 5,000 reports in 1955. They concluded that most sightings were common mistakes, such as weather balloons, solar reflections, and meteors. Only a small percentage could not be explained.

What was Washington's reaction to the UFOs? "Flying Saucers exist only in the imaginations of the viewers," stated President Dwight D. Eisenhower, December 16, 1954.

www.ingramcontent.com/pod-product-compliance
Lightning Source LLC
Chambersburg PA
CBHW031229260626
47169CB00007B/2221